One Last Life

Annika Sundberg

Published by BiblioBunny Books

Cover by 100 Covers

Edited by Carrie Gessner

ISBN-13: 978-1-7370529-2-0

For my mom.

And for Nikolai, my Chuck.

Chapter 1

Chicago, Illinois

Tristan cuddled down farther into his blankets, wishing he could pull his hands in with him. But even though he had no heat and no electric, he had work to do. By the light of the second-to-last emergency candle, he read an Arthurian spin-off from his e-reader. His review was to be in by Friday, and he preferred to read the whole thing at least twice before he wrote the actual article.

But the book was awful.

Re-reading was doing nothing to improve it.

He was tempted to throw the e-reader across the room, but that meant he'd have to leave his blankets to retrieve it, because like it or not, he needed the money that badly. Sure, for whatever reason, the paychecks from his company weren't coming, but there was some small hope that *this one* would arrive and then, he could eat. Or pay the electric bill so he could plug in his devices again.

Though paying the electric bill at this point wouldn't really fix the larger problem. The only reason no one was beating down his door to evict him was the day: Christmas Eve. Christmas was a time for caring, so his landlord would overlook obvious vagabonds like him who hadn't paid rent in far too long.

For a day or so.

The day after Christmas, though…he didn't want to think about that. Unless the review company found all the paychecks they swore were delivered to his home, he would be out on the street, a particularly daunting prospect for someone like him.

The candle flickered in some unfelt breeze, then a knock came at the door. He jumped in response, fear and resignation welling in him. They had come despite the holiday. At nine o'clock at night, no less. His first day on the streets would be a long, cold night instead.

The knock came again.

He'd best not make them wait. Otherwise, they'd break down the door and add the cost of the damage to the hefty bill for his overdue rent and utilities he already couldn't afford. Perhaps they would toss him in jail. At least jail would be warm. A nice change of pace.

But the thought of having to share his cell with another person made his skin crawl.

Tristan tried and failed to extricate herself from the blankets, so he got up and shuffled to the door, fabric over his head and trailing along behind him like a medieval cloak. He clutched the candle in his free hand, completing the look of Dracula welcoming Jonathan Harker to his home.

Tristan peered through the fisheye. An alligator in a blue business suit checked his watch in the hallway outside.

Nothing unusual there. He opened the door.

The alligator looked up and asked, "Tristan Harper?"

Tristan checked up and down the hallway before nodding. No cops. Alligator-man was alone. Now *that* was confusing.

"Good evening and Merry Christmas, Mr. Harper. I am from the law office of Arnold and Mack from Pittsburgh, Pennsylvania. I have a registered letter for you. Please sign."

The reptilian hand held out an official-looking paper. At the top, 'Arnold and Mack' glittered in gold embossing. Tristan took the page with the hand not holding the candle and attempted to read it. The alligator took it back immediately. Tristan hadn't even signed it. "Good enough, Mr. Harper. Enjoy your Christmas."

Alligator-man pressed a thick, white envelope into Tristan's hand, then turned and walked away.

Tristan watched the courier leave, his candle still held high despite the electric light of the hallway. There was something odd about that alligator-man and it wasn't the fact he was an alligator.

Tristan had seen things no one else saw all his life. His mother had brought him to the doctor when he was a child, and he had been diagnosed with a fanciful imagination, upgrading to audiovisual hallucinations in his teens, effectively cutting off any possibility of a driver's license. No one wanted to be the one behind the car braking for a herd of giraffes that no one else could see.

But the things he saw were very real. He was quite convinced there was nothing wrong with him, but his mother and society at large had disagreed, so he tended to avoid both, though after his mother's death, he regretted that avoidance a little.

He had learned long ago not to point out the fairies to anyone, but he constantly feared slipping up and showing how crazy he really was. One thoughtless comment on how shiny someone's scales were, and they would send him to an institution. He'd been in one for a short bit and didn't fancy another go.

He withdrew into the apartment that no longer was his, mysterious envelope in hand. It was absurdly heavy for an envelope of legal documents. He sat on his couch and drew his knees up to his chest, his stored body heat inside the blanket bringing feeling back to his chilled toes.

Pittsburgh.

He didn't know anyone in Pittsburgh. At least he didn't think so. He set down the candle and held the envelope toward it. It was blank. Just your average big, white envelope.

May as well open it.

He ripped open the top and pulled out the folded papers inside. The same golden letterhead as on the document he hadn't been allowed to sign glittered at him. He upended the envelope to make sure everything had come out and something heavy fell into his lap, thankfully not hitting anything important. Peering downward, he scrabbled in the folds of the blanket and discovered a large brass key, the old kind with only two teeth and an ornate handle. It was brown with age, like a piece of decorated chocolate.

What in the world?

He set the key on the end table next to the candle and took up the letter. “Dear Mr. Harper, we regret to inform you of the death of your great-aunt Tilda. On her death, as the last surviving beneficiary of her will, you have inherited Tilda Swinton’s last worldly goods, including a furnished home in Pittsburgh, Pennsylvania.”

The address and an itemized list followed, as well as an amount of money that seemed unbelievable.

The letter ended by asking him to come to the office of Arnold and Mack as soon as possible. There was no address for the office. He flipped over the paper just to make sure it wasn’t on the other side.

Nope.

But under the single-sheet letter was the deed to the house, all crinkly with age but utterly real with a paper-punch notary seal in the corner. His name sat on the “owner” line. The house was legally his. At least there was an address on the deed document.

In the sparse light of the guttering candle, Tristan looked around the overpriced one-room Chicago apartment he would be kicked out of in two days' time. He set down the letter and picked up the key. Well, he wasn't doing anything important tomorrow anyway.

Even though he was pretty sure he wasn't related to anyone named Tilda Swinton, and in fact he was certain Ms. Swinton was a British actress who was still very much alive, there sat the key.

To a house that he owned.

And if it turned out to be a very strange ruse, being homeless and alone in Pittsburgh would likely be just as pleasant as being homeless and alone in Chicago.

He picked up his smartphone and used the last of its battery and the last remaining money in his bank account to buy himself a bus ticket from Chicago to

Pittsburgh the following day. Perhaps his life was about to take a sudden turn for the better.

Merry Christmas to me.

He blew out the candle and flopped over on the couch to sleep. He would have plenty of time to finish reading the novel on the bus.

Bluish dawn light filtered around the edges of Tristan's light-blocking curtains. The curtains were supposed to block cold as well but were ineffective when there was no heat from the inside to counteract the outside temperature. His nose felt as though it had been replaced with ice in the night. He sat up, and the heavy key slid down his body to land in a *thunk* on the floor.

He took a moment to wonder how it had come to be on his person instead of the side table where he'd left it, but dismissed the inquiry. Stranger things had happened. Like the events surrounding the key's arrival. He burrowed back into his blankets, hiding from the inevitable. All of his late-night bravery had evaporated in the light of the new day, and he was no longer certain he'd made the right choice.

Pittsburgh.

He'd lived his whole life within a couple blocks. Pittsburgh seemed a world away. *Other* people lived elsewhere, not him. He had a mostly predictable life in his apartment alone. After a chaotic childhood filled with fearful glances generally reserved for those who may become dangerous, normalcy was all he craved.

But heading a world away with a mystery key was better than staying where he would end up on the street. His life here had stopped being predictable when he had no longer been able to pay his bills. It was time for a change, and some guardian-angel type had dropped his salvation directly on him. He wasn't one to squander blessings.

Decisiveness filling him, Tristan got up too quickly, his blanket cocoon flopping open and exposing him to the elements. He winced as his feet touched the cold floor. He was up now, and he regretted it deeply. But he went into his kitchen and grabbed the last of the granola bars that were the only food he owned. He munched on one as he changed out of his pajamas into something more suited for travel.

Packing was a simple matter. Tristan hated to leave behind most of his earthly belongings, but he supposed that his landlord could auction the items off so that he could reduce the bill, though he suspected that instead, the landlord would hire a dumpster and charge him for the removal of his stuff. But what was another bill in an already impossible pile of them? Maybe if the money was real, he could pay off what he owed. But the whole situation had an unreal quality he couldn't quite bring himself to believe in. An irony for a man who fully believed that sometimes, the Chicago mounted police rode unicorns.

He gently laid his electronics and some extra clothing into the backpack he used when he made the weekly trek to the bank to cash his checks and then to the coffee shop to force himself to socialize.

The letter and deed went in the protected pocket with his laptop, the heavy key into his pocket. He wasn't one for sentimental items, and it wasn't like he could move out the furniture, so he left everything else behind.

The letter said that Aunt Tilda's place was furnished. And if the amount of money the letter suggested actually existed, he could afford to buy new clothes. He wouldn't want for anything. But if he ended up on the street...well likely one bag of belongings would be all he could tote around.

He took one last look around. His blankets still sat in a knot on the couch, the stub of the candle he had used the night before cemented in a puddle of dried wax to the top of the side table. The place had been serviceable, a haven away from those who would put him in a box labeled with whatever mental illness they thought he had. With a little reluctance, he closed the door and locked it for the last time.

The elevator was out, as it always was, so he took the stairs instead, the dingy moldy scent now triggering nostalgia instead of triggering an almost overwhelming desire to clean.

On the bottom floor, he took his apartment key off his key ring and dropped it into the slot marked “keys” at the tiny, closed apartment office. He felt a little guilty not leaving a forwarding address, but if the promised money came through, he would just send what he owed with a return address then. If not, well, it’s not like he wasn’t already destined for jail.

He headed out into the cold, pulling up his jacket's hood. Ice sparkled on the ground, and snow flurries mixed with tiny ladies in white dresses swirled around him. It was Christmas morning, and Tristan and his tiny snow companions were the only people out and about.

The women followed him for a while only to drop off as he passed into places he'd never been before. He kept walking without them, going to the bus station that would send him away from home forever.

The bus station was dirty and unpleasant, but then again, so was Tristan. They were meant for one another. He went over to a self-serve terminal and printed out his bus pass, then checked the time on the analog clock, ticking dusty and unnoticed on the back wall, obsolete in the era of smart phones.

At noon on Christmas day, Tristan had the run of the place, so he was able to snag an uncomfortable plastic seat with an outlet nearby. There were only two ports and after a moment of deliberation, he plugged in his e-reader and phone. As little as he used his phone, it was still probably the most important thing to have charged during a ninteen-hour journey to a city he'd never been to. His cheeks went cold, and he had to take a few deep breaths to regain equilibrium.

To keep himself from thinking about everything that could go wrong, he pulled up his review book. It was still terrible but better than letting his anxiety get the better of him.

Twenty minutes and a partial charge later, the announcement for his bus buzzed over the ancient intercom, the male-like automated voice amorphous around the vowels.

Unplugging and rising, he readied himself. A few others had arrived and trundled to the door—an old man with Walt Disney hair and a waxed mustache, a short woman in a pink bubble jacket with her hood pulled up, and a tall man. But no, there had been no tall man there. Just one of those things he saw no one else did. A flash and gone.

People popping into and out of existence no longer bothered him. They had become the normal that existed only for him. Ghosts? Demons? Hallucinations? An overactive imagination like his mother suggested? It didn't matter anymore. For him, it was normal.

He handed his ticket to the man sporting a pair of large elephant ears standing at the door to the bus. The ears were impressive. Really too bad Tristan was the only one able to see them. Everyone else would think the bus driver looked like anyone else.

"Anything to check," the man shouted over the roar of the bus engine. Tristan shook his head and the man handed back his ticket, ushering him onto the bus. "Have a good ride. Nineteen hours is a long time. You'll be with me for the long haul."

The man gave Tristan a smile, his small tusks pulling his lips away from his teeth. Tristan forced himself to smile back even though he wasn't sure how he felt about a man with elephant ears driving him from noon to four in the morning. All by himself. He tried to remember if elephants were one of the many animals that slept more than they were awake.

He walked up the steps onto the bus and chose a hard, barely padded seat decorated with 80s-inspired magenta and purple paisley paint explosion fabric. The three others were the only others on the bus with him.

Ah. The tall man was back.

The scent of exhaust surrounded him from where it came in the open door, and he stared out the window into the gray, slush-covered city.

Should everything go well, he would never see Chicago again.

He was sure he could come to terms with that eventually.

Chapter 2

Pittsburgh, Pennsylvania, December 26

Tristan had dozed for a while, but the discomfort of the chairs and a distrust of others had kept him too wakeful for more. He glanced at his watch as the darkness of countryside gave way to streetlamps, far too brightly lit for four in the morning.

Few passengers had stayed on the bus long as they chopped through Indiana and Ohio in an efficient straight line then meandered aimlessly across Pennsylvania only to eventually turn around in a darkened box store parking lot and go back the way they had come. All in the sleeping dark of a land devoid of people.

He must have drifted off in the flickering light of the streetlamps because he woke to the sound of the breaks screeching just as they had every other stop. They were coming into a large, triangular parking lot, surrounded by a sea of nothing. Panic tickled the edges of Tristan's consciousness.

He had expected to arrive at a station not unlike that in Chicago: in a little neighborhood, surrounded by outlets into the world. But the ocean of parked cars around the small building belied that hope. He was going to have to find his own way out of the urban wasteland. He pulled on his bag as they rolled to a complete stop, his mind buzzing with doubt.

"Pittsburgh, Pennsylvania," the driver said into the old drive-thru-like overhead speaker, then disembarked, stretching his legs. Tristan followed, the cold air of the outside world rushing over him, slapping any lingering sleep out of his eyes.

“It’s been a good trip, eh?” The driver shouted over the rumble of the bus as he cupped a cigarette against the icy breeze knifing its way between the bus and the building. He looked tired. Tristan hoped this was his last stop for the night, for his sake. 19 hours with only tiny breaks at each stop was just too much for one man. Tristan gave him a smile, then escaped into the building.

Inside was warmer, but small. There weren’t many seats suggesting an optimistic attitude toward passenger turnover. This was not a place meant to be stayed in for long. At the back was a tiny commissary with a tired-looking woman with too much hair playing on her phone behind the counter.

In the other corner was a pay phone surrounded by posters for car-rental services. Helpful if he had a driver’s license, a shred of adventuresome spirit, or money. He sighed and dug in his pockets, hoping he had forgotten some errant cash that might just cover the price of a coffee and the fare for public transport to his new home or at least somewhere he could shelter until the law offices of Arnold and Mack.

Unsurprisingly, he found no cash, so he pulled out his phone. He knew he had wiped out the remaining balance purchasing the ticket to Pittsburgh but who knew, perhaps one of the missing checks made its way to his account in the night. He thumbed through his bank app.

Holy crap.

He looked around surreptitiously, hoping none of the people milling about had noticed his profound surprise. He stared at his screen again just to confirm it was not a hallucination.

Apparently, he didn't need to make it to the office of Arnold and Mack for the money to make it to him. It already had.

With a twist of frustration, he wondered if he wondered if he had waited a little longer, he could have stayed in Chicago where he was comfortable. Of course, a deposit wouldn't have gone through on a holiday. But he was here, and he couldn't deny he was curious. The money was real. The house could be real too. He may as well see it and get some real rest for the first time in a long time.

He sidled over to the ticket desk and asked, "Excuse me. Do you have the number for a reputable taxi service?"

The guy grunted and pointed at the wall with the posters.

Tristan shouldn't have expected more from a man with a fly proboscis instead of a mouth. The multifaceted eyes moved away from him, back to whatever was on his computer screen. Tristan didn't want to contemplate what a fly-man on an overnight shift would watch.

As Tristan walked back to the opposite end of the bus station, an older man caught his elbow and said, “Couldn’t help but overhear your question.” He handed Tristan a small flier. “It’s kinda like Uber but local.”

The older gentleman smiled and gave him two thumbs-up as though they shared a secret, then walked away, leaving Tristan holding the flier.

He glanced at the back wall with its ripped and graffitied posters then at the flier in his hand.

On the glossy surface, it outlined the need for safe taxi services because of the train, plane, and bus hubs in Pittsburgh.

“Steeling Cars” touted itself as this safe alternative to other unknown taxi services. It was an unfortunate choice of company name, so he googled it. The website looked reputable, and there was a little video endorsement from Tilda Swinton.

The coincidence was too much for him. He called the number.

“Steeling Cars,” the voice on the other end was female with an Irish accent.

“Um, yes. I was handed your flier at the Pittsburgh bus station, and I was hoping I could get a ride to my new house... Oh, and um, does your service use card-readers?”

“Yes, we do. We can get a car to you in five minutes. Your name?”

“Tristan Harper.”

“OK Mr. Harper, keep an eye out for a green Volkswagen Beetle.”

They both said their polite goodbyes and hung up, and a feeling of pleasant anticipation tickled the inside of his belly. This was really happening. He had money and a house, and everything was going to be okay after all.

* * *

The green Volkswagen Beetle arrived in under five minutes. Tristan stood from the bench outside the bus station, uncertainty trying to take hold of him again. A stranger in a new city could disappear quite easily and no one would know. He shook off his fear and shivered at the same time.

The driver's door opened, and a short redhead woman stepped out. She was less than five feet tall and had a soft, rounded face. Adorable and mischievous at the same time, Tristan could fairly see the shamrocks and pots of gold floating over her head like an invocation of all things leprechaun.

"Hello there, Tristan. I'm Fiona. I'll get you where you need to go," she said. The same voice from the phone.

Tristan hesitated. "Who's manning the Steeling Cars telephones if you're here?"

The small woman laughed, a musical sound. "Good ear. There's several of us.

Usually, whoever takes the call takes the fare if we're close enough. Which I was."

She waved Tristan forward and ducked into the car, popping the front passenger door from the inside. "Let's go. I'm not sure if you've noticed, but it's freezing out here."

Like a chastened child, he got into the car without even a thought. The vehicle was a little cramped for him but the perfect size for the driver.

He did not comment on the cushion that held Fiona up so she could see over the dash.

She looked over at him and said, "Where to?"

Tristan gave the address, and Fiona nodded. "A long haul from here. Swanky. You late to a Christmas party?"

"No. Inherited a house." He was glad to hear that the place was in a good neighborhood. He hadn't stopped to think too hard about the condition or placement of the home before. He'd put all his eggs into a basket that could be condemned and filled with squatters.

"Must have been hard to get such bad news on Christmas," Fiona said over the sound of the car's laboring heater. "She must have been pretty important to you if you rushed out on a holiday to sally her off to the next life."

Tristan shook his head. "Never met her. I was about to be evicted so I thought maybe this place would be better than the streets."

Fiona did not reply.

Obviously, Tristan was showing his weirdness again and his lack of social prowess. Normal people had family to be with on Christmas. They didn't condemn themselves to near day-long bus rides until the deep dark bits of the morning.

They drove along in silence, the sleeping five a.m. streets blinking at them in the light of the streetlamps, not ready to wake.

* * *

The car slowed, then stopped.

“Mr. Harper?” Fiona jostled him with a thickly gloved hand.

Tristan rubbed his grainy eyes. He hadn’t expected to fall asleep, but despite the driver’s stranger status, he had felt comfortable. Unusual.

“We’re here,” Fiona said.

Tristan looked out the window into the darkened street. Fewer streetlamps dotted the street. Enough to help drivers see, but not enough to glare into bedrooms at night.

“Um, do you mind if you wait for a minute? I’m not completely sure this key is real.”

Fiona laughed. "You're an adventurous one."

How wrong she was, but he didn't correct her.

She handed Tristan her smart phone with a little card reader at the top. "Put your info in now, and if you come back, I'll charge you for the time to a hotel as a separate transaction."

Tristan nodded, and though he had seen the balance in his account with his own eyes, he felt a bit of apprehension as the transaction processed.

Fiona gave him a smile. "Off you go. If you're not back in five minutes, I'll assume I'm leaving you here."

Anxiety beaded sweat on Tristan's forehead despite the chill wind seeping in through the partially open door. Before he got out, he said, "I'll come and tell you if I'm staying or not. It may take me a moment to try the key, and I don't want to be abandoned here if it doesn't work."

Fiona laughed. "All right, Mr. Harper."

Tristan started up the cracked concrete stairs from the sidewalk toward the house. A huge tree grew on either side of the front steps, masking the building's size, but he got the impression it was quite large.

The pitted walk led to the wooden porch steps, four in all. He went up the first and second, skipped the third straight to the fourth. Confused for a moment, he stopped, then put a foot on the third step. It creaked and felt a little less sturdy than the others.

How did I know to avoid it?

He pulled open the screen door of the enclosed porch. The floor creaked as he walked the few feet to the front door. A long-empty house often gave the impression of being abandoned, maybe even feeling a little creepy. But this one didn't. It was old and uninhabited, but it still felt like coming home after a long time away.

He shook his head and fished the large key out of his pocket, fitting it to the door. It slid in easily. With a twist and a click, the door was open. It was real. It was all real. He had a house in Pittsburgh and money enough in the bank to buy a small state. Just yesterday, he'd been wondering where his next meal would come from and how he would survive.

Outside, he heard the green Beetle pull away. Fiona hadn't waited for his go-ahead, but that was okay. Everything was finally okay.

He pushed the door open and flicked the switch to the right of the door and nothing happened. He gave a laugh. Well, he couldn't expect everything to be perfect right away. He could get the power on later. He had the time now.

He shut the door behind him. The moon's light illuminated an enamel-topped table and chairs as well as an old-fashioned refrigerator with a latch handle. Tilda hadn't been very up with the times. But Tristan could fix it.

In the morning.

Which it technically already was.

He passed through an open doorway from the kitchen into the living room and sat down on the first piece of furniture he found. The green wooden-legged couch held him and smelled fine, so he lay down. Tilda had kept the place in good condition even if her tastes leaned toward the archaic.

He pulled several of his shirts out of his bag and laid them on himself like blankets then let his backpack slide to the floor. Exhausted, he fell asleep in his new home, his mind free and clear for the first time in months.

Chapter 3

Pittsburgh, Pennsylvania, December 26

Sun filtered through the lace curtains, and a bird twittered loudly in a tree outside. Tristan woke unwillingly, his body aching from the cold. Moving his arms and legs was like snapping icicles, and his toes were chilled like uncooked chicken tenders.

Tristan sat up and rubbed his hands over his face and arms to get some feeling to return. First order of business was to get the utilities turned on and go find something to eat. He stamped his feet a few times and pulled out his phone. The battery was still good enough despite the incomplete charge in the bus station, for which he was grateful.

The letter from Arnold and Mack may not have had an address, but they had a phone number under their gilded names. They likely had been the people to turn off the utilities in the first place. They'd be able to tell him who to get to come turn it back on.

He typed in the number and let it ring before he even stopped to wonder what time it was. He hadn't even looked.

On the third ring, a male voice answered. "Arnold and Mack." The voice had a light Spanish accent.

"Yes, this is Tristan Harper. I came to inspect the property I inherited recently and have found that the utilities are off. I was wondering if you could offer me any information on how to get them turned back on."

"Ah, yes, so sorry for your loss, Mr. Harper. I can give you some phone numbers. Do you have a pen and paper handy?"

He did not.

"Ah, well. Give me your email address, and I will send them via email."

Tristan gave the man his email address and then asked, "Do I need to come into the office for any reason? I notice the money mentioned in the letter has already been credited to my account."

"No, Mr. Harper. No need. Taxes have already been taken on the inheritance, so you need not worry about claiming them come tax-time either. Oh, the mailman did mention some mail accumulating at the address. We had meant to come out to clear it, but you arrived so quickly."

Tristan glanced through the window toward the porch. "Oh. Yeah. I'll take care of it. Probably just junk mail. 'To current resident.'"

The man on the other end thanked Tristan, then said his goodbyes.

Tristan hung up and wandered through the kitchen to the front door. A little metal mailbox next to the door was bursting with envelopes, so many it could no longer shut. He opened the door, barely noticing the cold, and pulled all the mail out. The task took some tugging, but he got them all.

Bringing his haul inside to the kitchen table, he tossed them down on the table before he lost the lot of them. He picked up the first one. His name was in the window at the front, a familiar stamp at the upper left corner. A yellow sticker covered his Chicago address at the front, helpfully supplying the Pittsburgh address. An address he hadn't known until last night.

All his missing checks.

All his missing checks.

Tristan stepped back from the envelopes, eyes wide. Suddenly all the inconsistencies and oddities about the entire situation crashed down on him.

How had Arnold and Mack known his bank information to put the money into his account? How had that money appeared right after he'd left Chicago? Why send him the deed and key instead of making him come to the office to get them?

Tristan pulled out his phone and googled Arnold and Mack.

There was no such law office.

He googled Steeling Cars.

The web page that had given him the extra boost of confidence the night before no longer existed.

He sat down rather quickly, set his phone on the table, and put his face in his hands.

What in the world is going on?

From the table, his phone buzzed.

He picked it up and checked the notification. A new email from Arnold and Mack about utilities. He huffed a little laugh. So, they didn't exist, but they were ready to help him feel welcome in his new home.

However, in order to draw him here, they changed his address so that he would be utterly destitute. He couldn't quite figure out if he was on a reality television show, if they were from some strange charity, or if he would find a creepy puppet in the basement that wanted him to cut off his own leg.

Obviously, Aunt Tilda didn't exist. So, whose house was this? Would the actual homeowner show up and kick him out?

He sat, indecisive, for several moments, fear and uncertainty warring with a deep feeling of having come home. The place didn't feel like a horror movie. He had known to skip the third step on the porch stairs. Something was going on here, and he was determined to figure out what.

After he got some heat in the place.

* * *

An hour later, Tristan sat in his new living room, freshly washed and enjoying the warmth, such a luxury after the past few weeks. The water, electric, and gas companies had all been very obliging. None of those required a house visit, and they had been functional almost immediately. The internet company, however, scheduled an appointment to come sometime between 7am and 7pm a week later.

So that meant he would have to go find somewhere with free wi-fi to send out his work. He needed food anyway, so it really wasn't a huge deal.

Tristan wandered to the bathroom, tucked behind the stairs to the second floor. He finger-combed his auburn hair and pulled out the contacts he'd been wearing far too long. He'd have to put on his glasses for the trip, but it wasn't like he was trying to impress anyone. The way he would eat his first meal in over twenty-four hours may be more off-putting than wearing a pair of glasses anyway.

He had already taken a look at a map of the area on his phone and found a little shopping center a block away, complete with a coffee and sandwich place advertising free wi-fi.

It was brisk outside, but without the biting wind of Chicago, it was bearable. The sun dazzled off the snow, but it also warmed the shoulders of his black coat. At the sidewalk, he looked back up the rise to his house, light yellow and imposing in its Victorian-ness, and wondered if it would still exist when he got back or if it too would disappear into the ether like the website for Steeling Cars.

Tristan's stomach growled audibly, and he decided it was a risk he was just going to have to take.

He walked down the road, snow and salt crunching beneath his shoes. There were other homes along the block, just as big and just as old. One older gentleman greeted him as he shoveled the sidewalk in front of his house. It was strange to be in a place where people said hello to unfamiliar passersby instead of pretending they didn't exist.

No one else was out and about, even though he was still within a city. A rarity, but a welcome one. When at all possible, he preferred to be alone. No one around meant no chance of slipping up and accidentally making room for a large appendage that didn't actually exist.

The parking lot opened up before him, revealing thrift, grocery, and hardware stores along with the sandwich shop. Everything he could need in one place.

The parking lot was mostly empty, again a blessing. Everyone must still be recovering from the holiday. Or maybe, miracle of miracles, the stores just weren't that busy but still managed to stay in business anyway.

The heat hit him when he opened the café door along with the scents of soft, crumbly deserts, savory sausage and coffee. A moment of weakness passed over him as his stomach gave a great surging growl.

Few people inhabited the tables. Most of them were uninteresting, but his eye caught on a deathly pale fairy with weak, useless-looking wings sipping coffee with her companion, a hairy troll reading a newspaper.

Tristan walked up to the counter, eyes on the menu display above the register. When he looked down to the cashier, he rocked back on his heels. A beautiful black woman with blue streaks in her natural hair stood before Tristan. Her cheeks were pleasantly round and a little pink, showing maybe Tristan wasn't the only one too hot. He had never met her before, but he could swear she meant something deep and abiding to him. Just like the house, she was *right*.

Her rum-brown eyes widened, as though the same sudden overwhelming recognition had hit her as well. All the words he had ever known fled from him with glee as he lost himself in the stranger's gaze.

Amacy's morning had been slow and boring. Not many people were venturing out to eat while their refrigerators were still full of holiday leftovers and their wallets still held nothing more than dust from all their shopping. But then, the man from her dreams showed up.

Not the man *of* her dreams, but *from* them. She'd dreamt of his face over the years as they grew up together. She'd always assumed she had invented him, but there he was, standing in front of her. He was different from her dreams, less bold and decisive, but it was the same face.

The man was tall with shoulder-length auburn hair and thick, plastic-rimmed glasses. He was a little scruffy but wore a white button-down and slacks, with a black wool jacket overtop, showing he still had style. The outfit did not disguise his slim frame. His gray eyes riveted Amacy where she stood, and the look of awed astonishment on the man's face and a graceful stain of blush across his cheeks face told Amacy she wasn't the only one blown away.

Amacy's skin heated in embarrassment. She'd already been standing staring long enough for it to be seen as awkward. Her coworkers in the kitchen a few feet away would start to talk. She blinked, breaking their gaze.

After a deep breath, she asked, "What can I get for you?"

The man visibly regrouped and glanced at the sign above Amacy's head. "Can I have a coffee and a sausage croissant?"

Amacy pressed the buttons for his order with trembling fingers. *Jesus, Amacy, get hold of yourself. It's not like you've never seen a hot guy before.*

The man paid and wandered to the coffee station with his cup, looking dazed.

Amacy watched him go, wondering what pretense she could use to talk to him more.

Tristan brought his coffee and sandwich to a table in the front corner of the restaurant, large windows letting in lots of sunlight. He pulled off his coat and set his bag next to it, then stared at his breakfast for a moment.

He'd never had such a strong reaction to another human being before. He'd always assumed he was immune to the charms of the heart as he'd spent most of his life alone. Even in school when all the other kids were hooking up with one another and forming bonds that would last through the years of education they had together, he had stayed separate.

His stomach growled again, and base animal hunger won out against deeper consideration of the issue. He devoured his sandwich and glugged down his coffee in moments and silently chided himself for not ordering something larger. He hadn't been in full possession of his wits at the time and had just said the words of the first items he'd seen on the menu.

He thought about going back to order more, but he had acted like such a creeper he wasn't sure he could face the same cashier. Even if he wanted to, more than anything. He pulled out his laptop and started the arduous task of typing more about the book for review than "This book was awful. Do not buy it."

* * *

"Keep staring, and he might grow wings," said Jenna, Amacy's closest friend.

Amacy's cheeks heated, and she turned to face Jenna. "That obvious am I? I just can't seem to stop looking at him."

Jenna shrugged. "Tall and mysterious? Sounds like every straight woman's secret dream."

"I guess." Amacy couldn't put words to the strange feeling of recognition and some distant memory of deep and abiding love. It nearly took her breath away. But he was a complete stranger. She couldn't very well use the excuse that she'd met the man before in her dreams.

Jenna handed her a Styrofoam coffee cup. "How about you go offer him some coffee. On me. I'll pay for it. Just stop standing over here panting like a feral cat. It's breaktime for you anyway."

Jenna pushed Amacy forward and behind her, the till dinged then clicked shut as Jenna made good on her offer to pay. Amacy filled the cup from the same pump she'd seen stranger use earlier and walked over toward his table. His back was to the window, which was strange as most people who sat near the windows did so to look out. His hair sparkled more ginger in the sunlight. She had a sudden desire to run her hand through his hair to feel the warmth of his scalp and the sun on her fingers.

She grimaced. Best get herself under control before she got to his table.

He didn't even seem to notice Amacy's approach. "Hi," Amacy said, boldly sliding into the booth across from him.

He blinked and looked up. A momentary blush stained his cheeks. So, he must be feeling something for her as well, or maybe he was just really shy. Or in the middle of writing something completely inappropriate. She liked the idea of that.

"I thought you might want some more coffee," she said, setting the cup on the table. "Don't worry. It's paid for already."

She cringed at her own words, hoping he didn't take offense at the possible implication he couldn't afford another cup himself.

He smiled, a quick and adorable quirk of the lips. "Thank you. I was thinking of ordering another coffee and maybe some more food in a minute. You saved me from having to get up."

Relieved, Amacy smiled back. "You a writer?"

"No," he said, taking a sip of his coffee. His brows raised in surprise and he glanced up at Amacy, then looked back away. Probably surprised she'd brought the same coffee he'd had before. He must not have picked up on Amacy's too-noticeable-by-Jenna's-standards staring.

He set down the cup. "I'm a book reviewer."

Amacy nodded, trying to think of something else to give her an excuse to stay. “You new to the neighborhood?”

“As of yesterday. I just moved into a house I inherited from my aunt. It’s the yellow Victorian over on Braddock.”

Amacy’s eyebrows shot up, and she leaned across the table, hands out. “I love that house. I drive past it every day to get here.”

She’d been under the impression it had been uninhabited for a long time. She’d dreamed of buying it one day when she won the lottery or somehow got a better job. In her heart, it was home. Just like her unreasonable feeling of old love at the sight of the man across from her, she felt a nostalgic yearning every time she passed that house.

“Seems like a good place,” the man said. “I haven’t seen anything beyond the kitchen and living room yet.”

“Ugh,” Amacy said. “How can you stand being here instead of exploring?”

“Day job requires an internet connection, and your fine establishment provides that better than the house at the moment. They won’t be over to connect the internet until next week.”

Amacy’s heart swelled, and she couldn’t keep the smile from her face. “Guess I’ll see you a couple more times before you don’t need this place anymore.”

“Guess so.” The man’s full, kissable lips curled into a smile.

Awkwardness descended with the silence, and Amacy stood suddenly. “I better get back to work. Come visit me when you’re ready for food. I’m Amacy, by the way.”

“Tristan,” the man replied. A wonderful name.

Amacy walked away, certain she had said something she shouldn’t have or hadn’t said enough. At least she would see Tristan again.

Jenna raised her eyebrows as Amacy came back to the register. “So, when is your date?”

“I didn’t ask. I was too nervous.”

“I would go over there and ask for you but that would just smack of high school. Ask him before he leaves, or I’m disowning you as a friend.”

Tristan hit “send” and breathed a little more easily. Though he did not hurt for money any longer, he actually enjoyed what he did. At least when he only read books he thought might have actual merit. Which reminded him to look at the selections on for review for the next week. He would need to continue coming to the coffee shop to download the books and send his reviews for a while until the internet company could get his line installed.

The idea of going out for coffee every day seemed like an excellent one anyway. He glanced toward the counter. Amacy was waiting on an older lady with short gray hair and a pink rat's tail peeking out of the bottom of her skirt.

Tristan would go up and order something to go and then ask her about public transportation so he could find somewhere to deposit his checks and buy some bedding so he could sleep like a normal person. He hoped there was a mattress in the house that was new enough he didn't lie awake thinking he was sleeping somewhere someone died. Considering bed and sheet sizing boggled his mind so he considered maybe a quilt for now. Or a sleeping bag. And a pillow.

But he was having a hard time talking himself into doing so.

Though he had often been praised for his ability to craft a good review, speaking directly to real people with faces and bodies that may change at a moment's notice was not his forte. He steeled himself, ready to make some socially awkward faux pas that would make Amacy never want to speak to him again, and walked up to the register. He took care not to step on the other customer's tail.

The woman trundled off, the tail sweeping the floor behind her, and Tristan wondered how she kept it from getting cold in the snow outside.

He glanced up and noticed Amacy had caught him. He cleared his throat, hoping she didn't find anything unusual in his strangeness.

"I've come for food," he announced, an attempt to cover his weirdness with some silliness.

Amacy laughed and said, "Well, you've come to the right place."

Tristan ordered a tomato soup and cheese sandwich to go and delighted for a moment at the crestfallen look Amacy gave at the words “to go.”

“Before I leave, though,” Tristan said, “I was wondering if you might be able to help me out. I need to cash some checks and go somewhere that sells bedding, but I don’t know anything about the public transportation around here. Do you have a schedule or anything?”

Amacy checked her watch then reached under the counter. “I do have a bus schedule here, but if you’d like...” She paused as she handed over the bus schedule, her cheeks reddening. “I could drive you somewhere. I’m off in fifteen.”

Surprised, Tristan ran a thumb along the edge of the bus schedule. Social anxiety and a real opportunity to spend more time with a woman who seemed to never change appearance warred within him.

Amacy waved a hand at him. "Forget I asked. I'm just being over-friendly."

Her face had turned three shades redder than usual. His silence had made Amacy second-guess herself. Guilty he'd made her feel that way she said, "No. I would like that. Thank you."

An expression of relief crossed her face and Amacy said, "Oh. Good. Okay."

The buzzer she'd given Tristan to tell him when his food was ready went off in his hand, and he stared at it a moment before saying, "I'd better go get that."

He hustled over to the kitchen pick up but his food wasn't waiting for him. A middle eastern girl with tiny black horns peeking through her hair and a nametag that read "Jenna" give him a once-over with her eyes, then handed up his to-go bag with a grin.

"Be good," she said with a wink.

He blushed and hurried away.

Apparently, he and Amacy hadn't been very subtle if they'd drawn the attention of the rest of the staff.

* * *

It took Amacy three tries to swipe her punch card to clock out for the day. *Get it together, girl.*

Normally, men didn't have quite this effect on her. Sure, she'd felt excited for dates in the past, but none of them had ever felt so...important. As though the fate of the world hung upon her impressing *this* man.

Amacy took a deep breath. Clearly, she was psyching herself out. She was inflating his importance. He was just a super attractive guy living in the house she had always wanted and also happened to feature in her dreams at night. Forget the fact she had felt like she would have moved everything to be with him before he even mentioned the house.

“What is wrong with you?” Jenna touched Amacy’s shoulder as she leaned over to the time clock, startling her. “He is cute, but not *that* cute.”

“I don’t know,” Amacy said. “I feel drunk. It’s not even a date. I offered to help him buy bedsheets.”

Jenna smacked Amacy lightly with her purse and raised her eyebrows, waiting.

“What?” Amacy stared at her friend for a moment, during which Jenna waggled her eyebrows again.

Oh.

“Oh, my god,” Amacy said aloud. “He’s going to think I want to have sex. On those new bed sheets. Ugh. Way to up the stakes, Amacy.”

Jenna gave her a light kiss on the cheek. “Go ahead and keep pretending that’s not what you want. Your subconscious saved you there.”

And then Jenna walked out the back door and left.

Amacy ducked between the night-shift cashier and his boyfriend in the kitchen to get back out onto the restaurant floor. Tristan sat in the corner, his arm slung over the chair holding his bag and jacket, looking as though someone had clocked him right between the eyes.

He perked up as Amacy neared, giving her a bright smile, nearly knocking her dead.

"My car is in the lot behind the restaurant, but I figured I'd come out and get you and we'd go around rather than driving the car around so you wouldn't think I'd abandoned you." She was pretty sure she was babbling. She'd never done that before in her life. Maybe to try to get out of trouble with her mom, but definitely *not* over a guy.

He got up and put his jacket on. "All right."

“I figure we can go to the bank first. Pittsburgh is the town of banks. Our sports stadium is PNC Park after all.”

Tristan nodded. “I happen to use PNC, so that will be fine.”

They walked out into the blast of cold, though it felt good after the heat of the restaurant. It cooled the parts of her that were sweating more than they should. She didn’t zip up her coat. He walked very close to her as they traveled to the rear of the building and came to her brown Dodge Dart. The snow piled on the walk was the only reason she didn’t stare at him the whole time. She was so far gone it wasn’t even funny.

He startled her when he said, “I didn’t expect you to have a classic car. Not many people do these days. Must cost an arm and a half to drive.”

She shrugged. “I don’t have a long drive, so I don’t have to fill up often. My dad was into classic cars. This was his baby.

After he passed away, I made it my mission to keep her running. Both his little girls in one place." She didn't share that truth with many, and it surprised her how easily it had come out for him.

Tristan nodded and they got into the car. Unlike many older cars, her doors did not creak when they opened. And the leather on the seats inside was soft and unmarred. The old girl may have been her daddy's baby, but it was Amacy's baby now and she took just as good of care of her.

They buckled up and headed out onto the road.

A PNC was, of course, not far down the road, so she pulled in. It was still early enough for the bank proper to be open. Tristan reached into his bag and pulled out a stack of paper.

"Are those *all* checks?"

"The swanky life of a book reviewer. You're paid per job, not per hour, so you end up with a stack like this if all your payments for several months show up in one day."

"Your employer needs to get on the ball. Or you need to get direct deposit."

Tristan nodded, a rueful look on his face. "Direct deposit. I didn't think of that."

He got out and went into the building and since Tristan's bank information was an intimacy they hadn't achieved, Amacy waited awkwardly in the car. Three things a person was allowed to keep private until getting into a serious relationship—money, religion, and their past.

Though Amacy didn't really care about the first two, her dreams and their reaction to one another made her want to break her own rule and dig into Tristan's past. Had they met somewhere before? She couldn't figure out how else she would dream of the same man night after night.

She pulled out her phone to distract herself. She didn't want to think about this yet. Not while things were new. She didn't want to scare away the man she wanted to keep forever.

* * *

Tristan looked at the little slip the bank teller had given him, the amount of money in the balance line still completely foreign. And now it was higher because of two months' pay suddenly being added at once.

He could buy all the quilts he wanted.

He wandered back out and into the car, where Amacy waited, playing on her smart phone. This time, seeing her waiting, he didn't feel as nervous. Doing mundane things with her felt right, as though they had done little life-upkeep things together forever.

Getting back into the car, he said, "On to house things. And maybe a few groceries. I should probably eat sometimes when I'm not at the restaurant."

Amacy laughed. “That’s probably a good idea. There’s a grocery store next to a housewares store over yonder. I’ll take you there.”

They drove along in companionable silence.

He was the first to break the silence, his craving for more knowledge about her too strong to leave alone. “You lived here all your life?”

“Most of it. I was born in the city and grew up there. The only time I’ve spent outside it is when I went to culinary school in Punxsutawney. Yeah, I know. Went to school, and here I am a cashier at a coffee shop. It’s the American story these days.”

Tristan shrugged. “Sometimes you have to do a lot of work to use a degree. It’s certainly a lot easier to get a retail job.” He mentally added *if you’re a normal person*. And then wondered if he had come across condescending. Which hadn't been his intention.

"You got that right. You apply for a job in a kitchen, and they ask you what kind of menu you'd create. I love food, but I don't have the patience to come up with a whole menu. And of course, once they see me, they say, 'How are you going to keep all that hair out of the food?' Assholes."

Tristan frowned and agreed. "Assholes."

Amacy laughed. Tristan hadn't considered before that he maybe wasn't the only one in the car with whom society had issue just because he existed.

They went quiet again until they pulled into the parking lot. "Here we are," Amacy said, slipping into a parking spot and cutting the engine.

"Bedding first, I think," Tristan said, angling them toward the housewares store. "Come to think of it, I should probably get some pots and pans and cutlery as well."

The cupboards and drawers of the house had been bare. He thought of the old refrigerator.

“Come to think of it, I need a new refrigerator as well. Does this place sell refrigerators?”

Amacy shrugged. “Couldn’t say. The only time I’ve ever been in here was to pick up a wedding gift for a friend.” She turned a little to Tristan “You mind if I help you pick out your cookware? Gotta use my degree somehow.”

“Sure,” he said, unable to keep the smile off his face at Amacy’s eagerness. “I know nothing, so I could use a hand.”

They went in the front door and grabbed a cart.

Amacy was so excited to show off her knowledge they went to the cookware first. She picked out a set of pots and pans, then added a stock pot, and a wok, and a Dutch oven, and then looked up at Tristan and said, “I think I may have gone a little overboard. Everything in this cart together adds up to about what I make in a week. I'm sorry. I just get so excited I stop thinking about price tags."

She moved to take the stock pot back out, but Tristan pulled the cart away. "Not a problem. Let's go get crazy in the kitchen gadgets."

Amacy's face lit up, making Tristan's heart leap. "I love gadgets. Melon ballers and sauce mops. I could play in here all day."

"I don't know that I will ever need a melon baller, but go ahead and pick out anything an unaccomplished cook might need to make things taste right."

Amacy stopped and turned and looked at him, kitchen gadgets in each hand, and said, "How big is your kitchen?"

"I don't know," Tristan shrugged. "Bigger than my apartment in Chicago I think."

"Oh, god," Amacy moaned. "Please let me come and cook dinner in your kitchen."

"Absolutely. The appliances seem to be antiques, but I'm guessing they're functional."

"Old appliances... does that mean your stove is gas?"

"Yeah, I think so."

"I'm coming to live in your kitchen."

Tristan laughed, and Amacy continued to put spatulas and meat forks and temperature gauges in the cart.

"Now you need some dishes and flatware to eat with," Amacy said, pulling the cart and Tristan attached to it along with her. They entered the flatware aisle and were faced with all the patterns and sheens they could handle.

They perused for a few moments before they both reached out for the same set at the same time and laughed.

"I think this is a winner," Tristan said, putting it in the cart.

They whirled through the rest of the shopping and over to the grocery store for some staples.

They pushed all the items into the trunk, and Amacy turned to him with a laugh. "And here you thought you could fit all this on the bus."

She didn't mention that without her help, he probably wouldn't have bought so much.

"To the kitchen!" Amacy shouted as she slammed the trunk. "Can't wait to cook somewhere bigger than the tiny kitchen in my apartment. I can touch both walls. Normal-sized baking sheets won't fit in my tiny oven. A culinary nightmare."

Tristan got in next to her, a smile on his face. Just two days ago, he had been homeless and alone. And now he had a home and a beautiful woman who wanted to spend time with him in it. He felt thankful toward his anonymous benefactor who had gone to so much work to get him where he was.

* * *

They both skipped the third step on the way up to the house. Tristan didn't comment, and Amacy didn't seem to notice. The house was still there, which was good. It seemed that whatever strange plan the mysterious benefactor had, it included him having a house and money but did not include paying fees on websites he might only reasonably look at within a twenty-four-hour period. Someone who thought they were being sneaky.

He still couldn't understand why. He wasn't anyone important.

He pulled out his giant brass key and slid it in the lock.

Amacy made a truncated sigh of shock, her face dubious. "You might want to invest in some better locks with some dead-bolts as well. That looks easy to pick."

"Probably wise," Tristan agreed. He opened the door and flipped the switch next to the door, then picked up the big box of pots and pans he had set down.

"Oh, man, it's just as lovely as I imagined. Those windows over the sink—I love how they look out onto the yard."

"I have a yard?" Tristan peered out the window as Amacy laughed. "Maybe I should get a dog."

He'd never considered having a pet before. In his tiny apartment in Chicago, it just wouldn't be fair to coop up an animal like he did himself. But here, with a yard to play in, it might be a nice change from being alone.

The refrigerator opened behind him, and Amacy said, "I see what you mean about the refrigerator. Seems pretty cold, but it must be hell on your electric bill. Tomorrow's my day off if you want to drive over to Home Depot or Lowe's or something."

Amacy peered into the ancient refrigerator, and Tristan marveled at how despite only meeting this morning, they were already exceptionally comfortable with one another. Far more than he thought was completely normal.

Was Amacy part of the reason his benefactor had chosen this house? So they would meet? Nothing seemed unlikely anymore. When Alligator-man had handed him that letter, anything had become possible.

Amacy walked over to the stove and turned the dial. Nothing happened. No click-click of the igniter flashing, no scent of gas. "Whoops," she said, turning the dial back to its original position. "Guess there will be no cooking after all. Let's put all this stuff away. Dinner on me?"

"Sounds like a good idea. I'm starving just thinking about food."

They shoved the food into the refrigerator, then headed back out the door.

They skipped the third step on their way to the car.

Tristan smiled.

Tristan didn't generally like restaurants where dancing might happen, but he followed Amacy into the Lucky nonetheless. The restaurant had a bar on the far side of a large dance floor. Booths for eating customers lined the walls, tastefully separated from the dance floor by waist-high railing. The lights were low, and some customers already swayed to the music. A baboon danced with a very fine goldfish in a sundress.

The hostess led them to a booth where music played more quietly and the lights were marginally brighter. It had an old-fashioned feel as though it had been brought to life from a still in a '40s musical.

A waitress came over with menus and told them the specials. Old habits died hard, and Tristan ordered the cheapest thing on the menu. Mostly to get the waitress with waving octopus tentacles growing from her cheeks away from him before she turned him off his supper.

Amacy ordered as well, then said, "You sure were giving that waitress a weird look."

Used to explaining him problem away, he quickly said, "She looked so much like an ex-girlfriend it took me a little bit to realize it wasn't her."

Never mind that he'd never had a girlfriend, let alone an ex.

Amacy gave him an odd look but apparently accepted the answer.

A song with a Latin flare came on, and all but the baboon and his goldfish exited the dance floor, giving them space to show off. He tossed her in the air and whirled her around his body, her fins flapping wetly.

"I wish I could dance like that," Amacy said, an awed tone in her voice.

"They're doing surprisingly well," Tristan said, cutting himself off before he added, *What with her floppy fish body and his rangy baboon arms.*

"What's so surprising about it?"

Now he had dug himself a hole. He made a stab, hoping they were actual professional dancers and not just a pair out for fun. "Her shoes seem pretty precarious."

Amacy squinted. "I'll give you that. I wonder if they're professionals? I'd heard the Lucky employs them to encourage people to dance. I think I'd be less likely to dance after seeing them, though. I'm awful."

"Can't be any worse than me. I can't even dance as well as a fish."

He laughed at his own joke. That fish sure danced well.

The waitress came back with the food, and her arrival brought Tristan's attention to the back of the restaurant, where a short redheaded woman peeked out between the kitchen doors before quickly withdrawing.

He sat straight up. Fiona. The driver from Steeling Cars.

If the business had been fake, and she had ostensibly worked for it, had she been behind this strange sudden largesse?

"That woman in the kitchen," Tristan said to the waitress. "The redhead. Is her name Fiona?"

"Sure," the girl said. "Though to spell it, it sure doesn't look like Fiona. It's got a *g,* an *h,* and an *l* in it."

"Can I speak with her?"

"I can find out. But she's the owner, so I doubt she'll have the time. She rules the kitchen with an iron fist."

Tristan frowned. *She was just peeking out here, she's got the time.*

The waitress walked away, and Amacy gave Tristan a quizzical look. "That's quite the passion you whipped up about Fiona. Do you know her?"

"She drove the taxi that picked me up at the bus station." He stopped from saying more, then looked up at Amacy, wondering why he should. Unlike his illness, though the mystery was odd, it didn't reflect on him much. Except maybe his gullibility.

Normally, he would have waved off her question to cover up his own issues, but somehow, he knew he could trust her, that she wouldn't laugh at him.

"I think this whole inheritance thing is a sham. The lawyer who sent me the information doesn't exist. Someone had my paychecks forwarded to this address for two months so I was destitute enough to accept the promise of a house. The taxi service that got me from the bus station to the house doesn't exist, *and it was driven by that woman*. She's the only clue I have. I'm on edge because I'm afraid that the house and the money that I supposedly inherited from my aunt will disappear as easily as the lawyer and the taxi service."

"Damn," Amacy said, at this point leaning over the table in her excitement. "You have quite the mystery on your hands. If she doesn't come out and explain everything, maybe tomorrow, after we get you new appliances, we can search the house for clues. Figure out who owned that house."

Tristan somehow doubted Fiona was going to come out. And he wasn't about to get arrested trying to force his way in. "Maybe that's a good idea," he said with one last glance toward the kitchen.

He glanced up and found Amacy beaming at him as though he had just promised to buy a puppy and deliver it to her. His heart melted, and he thought of reaching across the table and touching her soft skin, but, certain that would somehow mess everything up, he instead applied himself to the chef salad.

Tristan got home late and slightly buzzed. They had ordered drinks and talked about insignificant nothings and wild theories of whose house he might have and how he might get Fiona to talk to him.

He left the lights off as he moved through the kitchen and living room to the staircase, grabbing the bag with the comforter along the way. He knew where everything was by now, and the light from the moon through the windows was enough that he could see.

As he walked through, though, he saw flickers and flashes of movement. No doubt headlights passing the house. But these shadows didn't move that way, in a logical path. Ghosts then, or hallucinations. The thought felt strangely comforting, as though he were no longer alone, something was no longer missing in his life.

He made it to the stairwell and tripped on the first rise, the moon's brilliance not reaching this far. He flicked on the light and started upward. He touched a scratch in the wall down near the floor and noticed another small rent through the top of the step. A dog? Inexpert handling while bringing up furniture? He couldn't be sure. The marks didn't look quite right for either. More scratches marked the wood as he gained altitude. How odd.

He came out on the landing and faced a hallway. A few doors stood open, and he passed them, unchecked. Tomorrow was for exploration. Tonight was for sleeping.

Tristan was drawn down the hall to the room at the end, and he walked into a room with a double bed held within the confines of a walnut sleigh-style frame. The rest of the furniture included a tall wardrobe, two dressers, and two bedside tables to match. The bed was dressed with a delicately-embroidered quilt, the pillow shams embroidered as well. His eyes ached a little as he looked at the tiny stitches, and he decided it was definitely too much alcohol and not the memory of eye strain.

He ran a hand across the blanket, worried it would be dusty, but his touch raised none. He turned out the light in the hall and stripped down to his underwear, climbing under the covers, abandoning his new quilt for the bedclothes already tucked in.

A light perfume like lilacs reached his nostrils, and he wondered if Aunt Tilda had come for a haunting for a moment before he realized the scent was quite familiar. It evoked nostalgia and yearning and without truly thinking about it, he got up and crossed the room, opening the top drawer of the far dresser.

He pulled out an old-fashioned atomizer and sniffed. Lilac perfume. He set the bottle on the top of the dresser and went back to the bed, confused. The alcohol in his body, however, smoothed the lines of worry and confusion, and he drifted off on a cloud into sleep.

A light jingling sound woke Tristan. The bed below him shuddered. It was as though he was back in the small apartment at the side of the elevated railroad tracks.

But he wasn't.

He got out of bed, and the floor tried to shake him back down. Car alarms went off up and down the street, and he could see lights flick on in the nearby houses. He picked up his phone from the bedside table and noticed the CNN app had pushed a notification to his lock screen. "Earthquake in Pennsylvania."

The shuddering lessened and then stopped.

He clicked on the story, but there wasn't much information yet, just the generic NOAA information that an earthquake had been detected. He set his phone back down, his body still shaking despite the earthquake having passed.

He took a deep breath, then lay down again. Sleep was not as elusive as he had expected.

Chapter 4

Unknown

Fire.

Everywhere.

Someone was crying.

He held out a hand to keep the panicking people from flooding forward. "No," he said. "Leave him alone."

The men around him looked as though they would argue, but they did not. He wasn't one of them, but he was respected and they wouldn't nay-say him.

He bent down and put his jacket over the reptile at his feet, a chubby-bellied red creature big as a Newfoundland dog, a long tail that ended in a spike, and two little useless wings at his back.

"I know you didn't mean to do anything wrong," he said to his companion, taking the creature's head in his hands and looking into the immensely sad eyes. He hugged him. "Come on now, Brassy. We have to leave. Not everyone is going to accept your existence. We need to hide you somewhere safe."

The dragon stood up, making a high-pitched squeaking sound he took to be a whine. Brasmanathnon knew what was coming. Even if the words hadn't been said aloud. He was going to have to go away. Forever.

Chapter 5

Pittsburgh, Pennsylvania, December 27

Tristan awoke with a gasp, grappling with the sheets for a moment before he understood he was no longer in the dream. Birds twittered pleasantly outside his window, and a few flurries drifted past the glass.

It was morning. There was no dragon. No fire.

He may as well get up and get ready for Amacy's arrival because he certainly wasn't going to be getting any more sleep.

As though to support his decision, his alarm started to jingle. He turned it off, the usual lock screen restored. More CNN news titles filled it, and he swiped to read them.

The worst earthquake in Pennsylvania since 1998. Focused at Centralia, PA. The fires that had burned in the town for decades burned even hotter, everyone in the town and nearby areas evacuated. No one had woken him to send him on his way, so he guessed Centralia must be a way away.

Tristan shook his head. Pennsylvania was far more eventful than he had expected.

He dressed and wandered downstairs for something to eat, and the same flickers he had experienced the night before were still apparent in broad daylight. His illness presenting a new symptom, probably triggered by leaving his comfort zone. Instead of his mind substituting or adding something that shouldn't be there, the new feeling was of something missing.

Something wasn't there that should be. An answer at least, even if a bit troubling.

He had reached the kitchen and grabbed an apple when his phone began to buzz. He pulled it out of his pocket and found that the number was labeled "Amacy" and was accompanied by a selfie of them together from the bar the night before. He didn't remember doing that and wondered what else he had done that he didn't remember.

He hadn't thought he'd been *that* drunk.

He swiped to answer. "Hello?"

Amacy's voice was full of excitement. "Hey there! Ready for our grand adventure today?"

With her words came a rapid sense of relief, of something broken having been fixed. "Absolutely."

"And do you mind if I borrow your sink before we go? The water main below my apartment cracked last night, leaving me without a means of brushing my teeth. That earthquake was crazy, huh? News says there was an earthquake in 1998, but I don't really remember it. And it was far more noticeable than that one in Maryland that barely quivered a few years back."

He recognized babbling when he heard it, but he wasn't sure why Amacy was. When she broke for breath, Tristan said, "Yeah, you can use my sink."

"Ok, cool, thanks," Amacy said and then was silent for a moment. "So, hey, before I hang up, silly question for you. Did you have any weird dreams last night?"

He most certainly had, but after years of prevaricating or minimizing his illness, he wasn't really sure what to talk about and what not to. Taking a chance, he said, "Yeah, I had a dream I had a pet dragon." He ended it with a laugh, hoping if it didn't correspond with hers, then his comment would appear flippant.

"Huh. Yeah. Me too," Amacy said. "Strange."

With a quick "bye," Amacy signed off, leaving Tristan stunned, still holding his phone against his ear in surprise. What was he to make of someone who had the same dreams?

* * *

Amacy found appliance shopping to be surprisingly quick and stress-free. Tristan had taken every suggestion she'd made, but she had begun to worry she was coming across as domineering.

She really wasn't.

But unfortunately for Tristan, so far, their interactions had centered on her passions—food and the things one needed to prepare said food. Kitchen stores were dangerous to her paycheck, so she tried as hard as she could to stay out of them, but Tristan seemed to be made of money.

That was kind of comforting and frightening both. Comforting because she kind of liked him and thought maybe if they ended up together, she might never have to live paycheck-to-paycheck again. Frightening because she had known him all of two days and she was already planning a future together.

The drive back to the house was done in silence; she worried about her own feelings, Tristan ruminating on whatever made his brain tick.

When they arrived back at the house, she spent some time daydreaming about what she would do with the yard space once it was no longer filled with snow. The front was sloped. A perfect place for a garden of plants with deep roots.

Stop.

She couldn't have the house just because she wanted it. Someone else was already living there, if for mysterious reasons. The bag of door locks banged into her knee as she unconsciously skipped the third stair to the porch.

Why did I do that?

She reached her foot back and tested the stair. It groaned and was uninterested in holding her weight properly.

She didn't remember feeling that in any of the other times she'd climbed the stairs.

Have I skipped it every time?

Looking up, she found Tristan looking at her.

He shrugged. "I do it too."

Amacy followed Tristan in and set the bags on the counter. To cover her confusion at their shared experience, she said, "We should probably move the old stove and fridge out from the wall before we start our search for clues."

"That seems like a good idea," Tristan said, inspecting the door and its handle. "Also, I seem to have a need to call a locksmith as I don't think the hardware we bought will be an easy swap with the existing ones. They're shaped differently."

"My friend's dad is a locksmith. I could call him and have him come take a look."

Tristan nodded, closing the door. He went to the refrigerator. "How long do you think the food I have in here would last if we unplugged this?"

Amacy laughed. "Just look outside. It's snowing again. Put it out there."

Tristan looked out, the look of fondness on his face unmistakable as he stared at the big white flakes.

Does it not snow in Chicago?

They moved the stove first. Upon moving it out a few inches, they discovered that it had not been hooked up to either the gas or the electric. "Guess you probably didn't need a new one after all," Amacy said apologetic.

"Don't worry about it. I read a news article once that said that gas stoves installed in the '70s or earlier could explode if you just tapped them. I'm pretty sure I'm remembering that wrong, but I don't know that I would feel safe with an old stove in the house."

They pulled as much as they could, then when it wouldn't budge anymore, Amacy climbed up on the counter and jumped down behind it. The space was surprisingly clean, as though someone had recently been behind the stove. Not a single dust bunny greeted her. Strange. For no messes to be present, that suggested someone being here more recently than she'd imagined.

She put her shoulder to the stove and pushed while Tristan pulled.

It moved the rest of the way out from the surrounding counters and onto the kitchen floor.

"You're quite strong," Tristan said.

“Can’t get through life too far skinny and useless.” Amacy regretted the words the minute she said them. Her mom had said the phrase so often in her childhood they’d lost all actual meaning. But Tristan’s tall frame had very little meat on it, and he could certainly take it the wrong way.

Tristan’s phone rang, and he stepped away to pick it up, leaving Amacy alone to worry she’d offended him. She climbed out from behind the stove and waited.

“The delivery men are headed over,” Tristan said, untroubled by Amacy’s comment. “Maybe we should empty the refrigerator now. We can put it back in the bags and put it all out on the porch.”

They went to it and were done quickly.

As with the stove, they grasped the sides of the refrigerator and pulled it out of its cubby a few feet before she climbed in behind and pulled the plug. There was no dust behind it either, but there was a square of paper on the floor. Her heart leapt in excitement.

“There’s something back here,” she shouted out around the fridge. “Scootch it out a little more so I can bend over. It’s unplugged.”

Tristan pulled and Amacy bent to pick up the square.

It was an old photograph in sepia tone. She thought it depicted a tall man and a woman in Victorian dress standing in front of the house, but there wasn’t enough light in the corner for her to tell. Suspicion spurred her, however.

She set it face-down on the counter, then announced, “It’s a photo. Let’s get this fridge out of here so we can see it better.”

They pushed and pulled, and as soon as there was enough space for her to get out, Amacy brought the photo to the window and nearly dropped it.

Her own face smiled out of the photograph at her. She had an arm around Tristan, their heads leaned toward one another in a cozy pose. She flipped it over. On the back, it said “William and Alma 1907.”

Tristan came up behind her, and she handed it over wordlessly.

He stared at it with a look more of resignation than surprise. “What do you see in this picture?”

“It’s you and me,” Amacy said, amazed. Why would he ask that?

Tristan sighed and handed the picture back. “Well, at least you and I are seeing the same thing. But in this case, that is not completely comforting.”

“I don’t understand,” she said.

Whether he deliberately misunderstood Amacy’s question or not, Tristan neatly sidestepped it, “I don’t know how this ended up here either. It’s obviously not doctored. This is a real antique photograph. Of people long dead if the date on the back has anything to do with it."

Amacy stepped back, troubled. The familiarity when they met. The deep love for the house. It all made sense if she believed in past lives.

But she didn't. Someone was obviously playing a very strange trick on them. Whoever gave Tristan this house wanted the two of them to end up together and suddenly, despite thinking about a possible future together mere moments ago, she wanted nothing to do with it. She didn't like this.

"I think I need to leave," she said, pressing the photograph into Tristan's hand as she turned to go.

The Christmas tree had been perfect this year, she thinks as she walks into the kitchen to begin the dishes. She'd hate to take it down, but in a few short days the thing would become a fire-hazard and with Brassy, they couldn't have that. She unbuttons the wrists of her sleeves and rolls them up as she turns on the water to fill the sink.

Amacy gasped and stumbled backward. Judging on the star-struck look on his face, Tristan had seen something too.

"I've got to go," Amacy said. "I'll call the locksmith for you."

Tristan nodded. "Thanks for helping me."

Amacy fled down the stairs, skipping the soft stair out of habit.

Amacy sat on her couch in her sweats, the television on but her attention elsewhere. She couldn't get her mind off the photo. Her face, though she wore garb more suited for the turn-of-the-century, her hair in braids like she hadn't worn since she was a child. With computers, people could do just about anything. Tristan could have photoshopped her face onto an old photo and printed it out. But could he really make the photo believably old? Amacy had seen photos of her grandmother as a baby and her grandmother's father's college graduation photo. You couldn't fake that kind of old. Not to her knowledge anyway.

So that left...what? Reincarnation? Lost memories? She...she just couldn't accept that. Nothing inside her had ever believed that kind of thing was real.

But why would she have skipped that step every time she'd been to that house? Why had he been a fixture in her dreams since she was a child? And why, when she met Tristan, did she know she loved him?

There it was. The truth. She already loved him. After knowing Tristan for slightly over twenty-four hours. But she loved him with all her heart. That wasn't Tristan's fault.

She groaned and curled herself into a ball. Amacy couldn't ignore that Tristan had been as surprised as she had over the photo, though his had come out as dismay rather than fear. Did the idea of being with her dismay Tristan?

Amacy laughed. What a stupid worry. She was obviously deranged, worrying about Tristan's feelings toward her when the larger problem was the photograph. Had she really accepted its existence so easily?

She picked up her remote and pointed it at the tv, raising the volume. "No casualties. However, the town of Centralia has lost its last 10 residents through relocation when the ground opened itself up beneath the church. The church did not survive." The news show showed the devastation, the crack through the ground, filled with flames. If there was ever any image that seemed to depict Milton's Hell, it was the one before her—the two halves of the church, barely standing on either side of the rift. “Burning continuously since 1962, the fires show no signs of stopping in this new development, but instead seem to have gotten stronger.”

Something about the situation chilled her to her very soul, but she couldn’t figure out what.

She turned the sound back down and tossed the remote to the couch. She didn’t want to be alone.

She thought of calling Jenna, but when she dialed the phone, she found the voice on the other end of the phone wasn’t hers. Tristan had answered.

Before she could stop herself, she said, “Hey. Do you want to go get drunk while we think about what that photo means?”

“Sounds perfect.”

“Pick you up in ten.”

She went to change out of her sweats.

* * *

Tristan got in the car and if Amacy had hoped that she would feel comforted in his presence, she was very wrong. An awkward silence descended between them as she drove toward the Lucky Bar and Grill. The bar hadn't been a conscious choice, but the location seemed to stand the most chance of getting them some answers. Fiona seemed to be a part of this, but an uncertain cog in the wheel of the mystery.

Even if all this turned out to be a very weird television show. "Surprise," Fiona would say. "It's a new fad, get matched up with a stranger we've convinced you is your life-mate beyond the constrains of one life alone!"

They pulled up to the restaurant and went in. They were seated in the same booth by the same waitress. She went through the list of foods on special, and as one, Amacy and Tristan ordered the second special, baked haddock and fries, with no hesitation. They looked at one another and blushed.

"I'm going to need something fruity with an umbrella and copious rum as well," Amacy added.

"Make that two," Tristan interjected.

The waitress raised her eyebrows and clicked her pen as she pushed her order wallet back into the pocket of her apron. "'Kay, guys, that'll be out in a few minutes."

Alone once more, they avoided each other's gaze.

In the background, over the bar nearby, the news shouted out more information about Centralia. Apparently, the smoke was toxic and more areas around the town were being evacuated until the flames could be controlled, though there was no guarantee they would succeed.

“I wonder what caused the earthquake,” Tristan said, turning back around to face Amacy. “I was always under the impression that Pennsylvania was pretty stable.”

“It is,” a female voice, Irish-accented and dour.

Fiona set a pair of plates in front of them, the fish still crackling with heat. She sat in the space next to Amacy as the waitress delivered their drinks. Three pink frothy fruity drinks with an umbrella in them.

“Strawberry daiquiris, my favorite,” Fiona said, taking a sip of hers. “Pennsylvania is very stable. Until a long-lost dragon decides that maybe it wants to leave the home it found for itself in the mines below. And that is exactly what is happening. William, Alma, Brassy is back, and it’s up to you to finally fix your mistake.”

Amacy stared, openmouthed at the woman next to her. First the photo, now this. There must be cameras everywhere. Fiona even used the names from the photo.

"Come on. We can find another bar," Amacy said, ready to push Fiona out of the way if she had to. To emphasize her point, she reached across the table and grabbed Tristan's hand to pull him along with.

A fat red dragon pulls itself up the stairs in front of her. "Brassy, no! You can't go upstairs. We'll never get you down again. Why do you always do this when Will's at work? I can't stop you anymore."

She reaches down to wrap her arms around the creature to pull him back, and he succeeds in pulling her off her feet before their combined weight sends them tumbling down the stairs. As they go down, his claws reach out and scratch the walls. They land in a heap at the bottom, Alma bruised and Brassy atop her. "You're just too heavy now. And too big to be a house pet. I don't know what to do with you."

Amacy sat down hard and found Fiona wiping up her spilled drink with a towel. Tristan, across the way, also looked dumbstruck.

Amacy couldn't stand it anymore. "What the hell did you do to us?"

Fiona raised her barely there eyebrows and said, "Well, nothing. Beyond care for your house and holdings until you came again. And maybe help you along a bit to find one another. Usually, we let you do that on your own time, and you probably would have soon, but if you haven't noticed, we're in the middle of a bit of a crisis. Every time it's harder to wake your memories, and I was hoping we had more time. But it doesn't seem to be the case."

Amacy snagged Tristan's cup as her own had suffered a catastrophic loss and took a long, brain-freezing drink before setting it down again. With a numb mouth, she said, “What the actual fuck?”

Fiona laughed, then got up. “I think you’ve discovered how to go about remembering. Keep doing what you’re doing, but don’t take too long. You know where to find me.”

She walked away, perfect and tiny and childlike. Obviously not nefarious. “She’s like an evil leprechaun,” Amacy said.

“You know that’s less insulting when it’s true,” Fiona shouted over her shoulder with a laugh.

Amacy gave a guilty jump.

“Well, now what?” Amacy crumpled into her seat, holding the drink like an elixir of life.

Tristan reached over and grabbed Fiona’s abandoned drink, plucking the straw from it, replacing it with his unused one. “That is a very good question,” he said, taking a sip.

* * *

Tristan watched a warthog wearing shorts and a tee draw his date out onto the dance floor while he framed his thoughts. He didn't want to damage poor Amacy more than she already was.

For someone who took life as she saw it, it would have to be difficult to suddenly realize she'd been seeing everything wrong. Tristan had been through the same as a child when his mother had him tested and was told that no one else saw the things he did. He had to tell her why none of this bothered him as much as it bothered her before she came up with her own explanations.

"My entire life, nothing has ever made sense," he said.

Pointing out onto the dance floor, he said, "That guy right there, he's a warthog. He's a pretty good dancer for having those little hooves."

Amacy peered over at the guy in question. “His high sides flat top and his extra chin do make him look kinda like a boar, I’ll give you.”

Tristan smiled at Amacy’s attempted commiseration as he swirled his pink drink in his glass. If he looked up, he was terrified he’d see the rejection in her eyes he always saw when he messed up.

But he had to continue. “I’ve lived my life being told that something was wrong with me, and suddenly, today, I have to wonder if it wasn’t that something was wrong with me but the world. With you, I’m normal. But now the world is messed up. What an exchange.”

Amacy furrowed her brow and chewed on her straw. “So, you can just... accept this? The dragon? The past life? The...fact that we’re meant to be together?”

“It’s difficult to disbelieve when you experience it. I had thought that the photograph was something my mind put there, but you confirmed what was there. I thought my first dream about the dragon was another hallucination until you said you'd had one too. And just now, I know you had some flash of the past as well.

"No one has ever seen the things I see. Except you. Let's work on the things we can work on and the rest, well, whatever happens, happens. Just because we were married in the past, it doesn't mean that we need to be again."

Fiona's words echoed in Tristan's head when he said it, though. Usually, they found one another on their own, without help. Maybe they would have found one another again, though it seemed unlikely since he would never have come to Pittsburgh on his own.

As though thinking along the same lines, Amacy said in a quiet voice, "My brother is getting married in Chicago next month."

Tristan raised his brows and said, "I was invited to a distant cousin's wedding next month as well."

Suddenly agitated, Amacy pulled some cash from her pocket and set it on the table. "This is for my meal and bus fare home. I gotta go."

She set down her drink and fled.

Tristan really wished she'd stop doing that.

He sat alone sipping his drink until the waitress came with the check. He paid, then left, feeling her pitying eyes on his back.

It was a quiet, empty night, and he was pretty sure he knew his way home. It wasn't far. People relied on their machines too much, their cars, their map apps.

He shoved his hands into his pockets and started walking.

Snow began to fall, glinting in the light of the streetlamps. Turning, spinning, dancing. They reached out their tiny fairy arms and swirled around him, dancing like beautiful ballerinas.

One came to his ear and whispered, “If he gets out, he’ll melt us all and we will never return. Will you save us like you did before?”

Man, my hallucinations are getting specific.

Unless of course, they actually weren’t hallucinations. Wouldn’t Mother just love it if she knew that fairies might be real? Or at least leprechauns and dragons.

Tristan turned a corner or two and discovered that he had thoroughly lost himself in an unfamiliar city.

The snow fairies zipped and fluttered before him, and as the snow became heavier, a green cat stepped out into his path and meowed.

"He knows your way home," said a fairy, then zipped away.

May as well follow a green cat through the streets of Pittsburgh. He could only hope that the cat knew he had moved and didn't try to lead him all the way to Chicago.

The infomercial guy had nothing to tell Amacy. He was far too shocked at how well the product he was showcasing did at its job. That plastic freezer bucket obviously had magic powers; he was so enthralled with it.

"I just need someone to tell me what's going on," she said to the muted infomercial guy. She wrapped herself in a blanket, leaving just her face exposed, and stared at the screen. The infomercial guy thrust the plastic freezer bucket at the screen, and the price popped up in the corner.

"Why is this happening to me? Yeah, I always wanted an interesting life, but I never wanted someone to just set it up for me, to make it so. I wanted to travel, eat snails in Paris. Normal kinds of interesting and adventurous."

The action on the screen went back to people failing completely to use plastic food storage buckets properly. They spilled soup, dropped buckets, and filled them too full. "I get how you feel, guys. My life is completely out of my own control as well. I always thought I'd choose to take a great job or find the perfect partner on my own. Some stranger wouldn't thrust me into a relationship with a person I've only known for a few days."

Together forever.

Meant to be a thing.

"'And by the way, total crazy just drips from my mouth when I talk 'cause you two must take care of a dragon.' Whatever the hell that means."

She groaned and rolled over, her feet popping out the end of her blanket burrito. "But no one made me dream of him. And no one made me love that house. Those were both me. And as much as I hate to admit it, I don't think it's possible for someone to force that kind of vision I had. There just isn't technology like that, and drugs wouldn't trigger upon touching someone, and there would be no guarantee that they would show me what the person wanted."

"Infomercial guy, you're supposed to be on the side of cold logic. Why are you trying to convince me that this completely illogical thing is real? There's no such thing as past lives. There's no such thing as dragons. Stop making me come up with rational reasons why what I saw was probably true."

She reached down and pulled off her sock and threw it at the television.

The infomercial guy gave her a huge thumbs-up and a smile.

"Ugh, even you're being creepy now."

Amacy lay back, facing the ceiling. "Damn me though. I'm too curious not to try to find out what's going on. It's not like I have to marry the guy or give him my heart completely. I know that this situation doesn't make any sense, and I can stay outside of that part at least."

She fell asleep convinced of her correctness, completely ignoring the facts that she was already in love, which the visions made harder to deny.

That night, she dreamed of Tristan unbuttoning her white wedding dress. She felt the kisses along her skin as though they were real. And all the good stuff beyond that. She couldn't be completely certain if it was a fantasy her brain had invented or something trying to pass itself off as a memory. It was the first time she hoped what her brain had showed her was a memory because the sex was damn good.

And in the morning, on her drive to work, a troll opened the door in the Squirrel Hill tunnel and waved to her from the raised walkway. And she didn't crash her car because part of her had expected it.

Chapter 6

Pittsburgh, Pennsylvania, December 28

Tristan decided to spend his morning in, telling himself the decision wasn't because he couldn't gather the courage to go near the coffee shop after Amacy's second sudden exit. A call from the cable company moving up his appointment between seven a.m. and noon that day cemented his choice.

So, he puttered around the downstairs, sweeping floors and dusting furniture. There was an old broom closet off the kitchen still full of cleaning supplies that looked mostly unused and rather new. So, he cleaned. And when he was done with the downstairs, he hesitantly climbed the scarred stairs to the second floor, sweeping them from top to bottom. There was barely any dirt, but it gave his hands something to do as his mind swirled.

His life had a purpose. Beyond forcing himself out of hiding to face the strange things he saw, hoping that someday, he could pass for normal. Amacy hadn't any inkling there was anything wrong with Tristan until he had told her. With her, the hallucinations were easier to ignore, gave him less anxiety. But was his admission what had sent Amacy running the night before? A cold sweat broke out along his hairline. Maybe she could accept the idea of past lives, the idea of a mission, but couldn't accept that the man meant for her was broken.

He swept under the bed with more force than the task really required. A strange *zip* sound told him he had snagged something. He pulled the item the rest of the way out and found that it was a yellowed plush photo album. On the front, William and Alma, the people in the photo from the kitchen, smiled back at him in their wedding finery.

He sat down with his back against the bed and flipped through the pages. Friends and family surrounded them, but the two in the most photos were Fiona and a tall Latino man whom Tristan was certain he had seen before somewhere, but couldn't place.

Will and Alma kissed, Alma's head tilted to the side, the little white top-hat with sprigs of white-painted holly on it tipping precariously, the only thing that seemed to hold it in place the veil weighing it down behind her back. Will wore a black tuxedo, the dark to Alma's light.

Tristan stared at the photograph and felt a painful longing in his soul. It had been so long.

A knock came at the door downstairs, and he jumped, scraping his leg against the bed frame.

He put the album on the bed and hurried downstairs to find the cable guy standing outside the kitchen door, tools at his belt, a cardboard box in his hand.

Tristan turned the handle and opened the door. “Come on in,” he said.

The man said, “Where you want it?”

“I found a cable-jack in the living room,” he said, leading the terse cable guy into the house, his insides bouncing painfully as he tried to keep his excitement and impatience under control.

He had looked so forward to getting the internet, and now it was an annoyance. It kept him from going back to look for more.

The man took up his spot and opened the box, pulling out the wireless modem. Painfully slowly, he pulled out the cable and the plug and plugged it in. Even more slowly, the lights came on one by one.

"Gotta make a call," the guy said.

He pulled out a large device that looked as though it had survived since the '80s and dialed. He had the volume all the way up, and Tristan could hear the entire exchange perfectly where he sat on the couch, but the guy still held it pressed to his head as though he could not hear otherwise.

Finally, he got up off his knees and came over. He held out the phone device and a crude stylus. "Sign it."

Tristan did so, and the man carried the box to the door.

"Where's the next one," he said into the phone as he pulled the door closed behind him.

Tristan didn't hesitate, running back upstairs to the bedroom.

He peered under the bed and found a flat cardboard box. He lifted off the cover and was not surprised to find the yellowing silk wedding dress from the photos, the small top hat crushed flat at the top. He pulled the hat out and popped it back into shape before setting the lid back on the box. Who kept their wedding dress in a cardboard box on the floor? It had obviously been put there for him to find.

He straightened and looked at the dressers and wardrobe. He hadn't opened them except when he found the perfume.

He threw open doors and drawers and found a couple other items—a box of jewelry, the suit, a comb, and a powder box. He touched the suit. It had been hanging in the closet, and he could tell by looking at it that it would probably fit him. On impulse, he stripped down and put it on. It was a little scratchy in places but still fit very nicely.

Wearing a hundred-year-old tuxedo, he left the bedroom, intent on searching the other rooms on the floor. He glanced up at the ceiling, noticing a hatch there. There was an attic above. And most likely a basement below. He would get answers. All the answers he could stomach.

But then another knock came at the door. Probably the locksmith. He quickly went back to the bedroom and changed out of the suit into his normal button-down and slacks. No need to show visitors how odd he really was.

But instead of a locksmith, she found a very contrite-looking Amacy holding a paper bag and two paper coffee cups.

“Can I come in?”

“Of course.”

She came in and set the food and drinks on the table. “Forgive me?” she asked.

Tristan waved a hand. “Nothing to forgive. I’m used to weirdness. You’re not. Of course it’s scary.”

She nodded. “I think you infected me. A troll waved to me in the Squirrel Hill tunnel today.”

Tristan raised his eyebrows. In all the years he’d had this illness, no one had ever admitted to seeing things like he did before. He relaxed a little and laughed. “I didn’t know hallucinations were catching.”

Amacy looked up at him, rum-brown eyes serious. “Unless they aren’t hallucinations.”

Tristan almost felt like the words were a punch to the gut. No, they weren’t bad words. Not bad at all. But the thought that someone believed him, thought he was telling the truth, and maybe wasn’t sick on top of that, made him want to fall to his knees and weep at Amacy’s feet. In that moment, all the other moments of desire and memory notwithstanding, Tristan was Amacy’s forever and ever.

* * *

Tristan led Amacy up the staircase to the floor above. Amacy traced some of the higher scratches in the wall of the staircase with her fingers.

Shit.

They corresponded to where she'd dragged Brassy downstairs in her vision.

She followed Tristan along the hallway upstairs to the room at the end, the light from the window across from the door beckoning them to enter.

The room looked just as it had in her dream the night before. Perhaps a memory then. She smiled. Atop the bed sat a photo album, a box with a wedding dress, an empty powder box, a perfume bottle, a box of jewelry. Behind her, the wardrobe was open. In it hung an old tuxedo.

She sat down, enveloped by the scent lilacs. There hadn't been many lilacs in the neighborhood where she grew up, but every time she smelled one on the spring breeze, it made her soul happy. She picked up the atomizer and spritzed some on her skin. The liquid was cold but made her feel whole for the first time in a long time, as though she hadn't really been presentable until just then.

Picking up the book, she looked through the pages. "Fiona," she said. "Is there some way to explain this all away? Say that somehow, she's drugged us or influenced us in some way to make this all happen?"

Tristan shrugged. "It does seem as though some of the things were planted, like the dress and the wedding album. And the sheets were sprayed with the perfume. But I knew exactly where to find the bottle. I don't know how she would make me do that. And if she were trying to convince us, why would she put herself in the photos?"

Amacy shook her head. "She looks the same. She hasn't even changed her hairstyle. Tell me something. Why would she remember more than us if it were real? If we've all been reincarnated over and over throughout the centuries, why would she be reborn knowing and we wouldn't?"

"I've been wondering that too."

"What if," Amacy started hesitantly. "What if she hasn't been reborn? She looks *exactly* the same. We look similar enough to get the drift, but for her, this photo could have been taken yesterday."

Amacy set down the book and reached for the dress box. She took the hat off the top and found that the bodice was buttoned down the front with little white buttons. It too was the same as her dream the night before. Her face heated immediately, and she glanced up surreptitiously to see if Tristan had noticed, but he had picked up the photo album and was looking through it.

Nothing happened when she touched the yellowing lace and silk of the dress. So, memories only came from other people, not from objects. She would have expected anything that she'd had strong emotions around would carry that with it, like a wedding dress. Maybe the memories degraded over the years.

But then how had they both had the first dream since they had not been touching? The dream about the dragon the night of the earthquake?

Nothing made sense.

"I haven't searched the other rooms yet. Or the attic. Or basement. Would you like to join me?"

Answers. She would love some answers. "Yes," she said.

Tristan held out his hand to help her up off the bed, and Amacy hesitated. She looked up into Tristan's eyes and saw he realized what he was doing. If they touched one another, they would see more. And he seemed to be all right with that.

She took his hand.

* * *

Will runs his hands down the back of Alma's neck and pulls her into a kiss. She responds favorably, and Will can feel the hunger behind her response. It has been so long. They've been so busy with the little dragon they've barely touched one another in months. He reaches down and pulls her hips against his own, the strength of Alma's muscles apparent even through the layers of fabric. Will wants her.

The little dragon barrels through the basement door, exploding it completely off its hinges. They part in surprise. Brasmanathnon runs across the kitchen and nuzzles his head against his master's leg.

Will sighs. How much longer are we going to be able to keep him? And what are we going to do when we can't?

* * *

Tristan flashed away from the vision only to realize that his body had apparently taken advantage of his vacancy and had pulled Amacy up against his chest.

Amacy gasped and looked up into his eyes, coming back to reality herself. They quickly broke away from one another. Tristan turned swiftly, the vision having left him in a state that confused him. He hadn't realized he could be sexually attracted to anyone else. Images others found sexy, he found bland. But now, he had found someone who had engaged his libido. And he wasn't sure what to do with that. After all, in this life, they still barely knew one another.

He headed down the hallway to the first of the other two rooms on the upper floors and opened the door. A small library with a desk at the center had been hidden within. He would have to bring his computer up. It seemed like a pleasant place to work. Someone else had thought the same, as an old typewriter sat atop the desk, the light from the windows behind illuminating the keys perfectly.

He wandered to the bookshelves, Amacy right behind him. He glanced over the titles, and his brow began to furrow. If there was one thing he knew, he knew books. He pulled down a volume to check the date inside and his suspicions were confirmed. He went to the other side of the room and inspected the other shelves as well.

Finally, he turned to Amacy, who was watching with a curious expression.

"None of these books is newer than the early 1970s."

She raised her eyebrows, a silent prompt to go on. "If Will and Alma were married at the turn of the century, let's assume that they were young, maybe 18-19. That's a pretty normal marriage age for that era. 70 years later, they would be 80. What if...

what if the last people to own this house... were us?"

Amacy's eyes blinked then went far away, seeming to consider everything. No doubt with her preoccupation with food preparation, she was thinking of the old refrigerator in the kitchen. Someone else would have surely replaced it by now, the energy hog it would be.

"And who would have taken care of it while we were busy being dead?"

"I think that's an answer only Fiona can give us. I think we need to go pay her a visit again."

Amacy frowned, but then nodded. "I think you're right. I don't like her at all, but I think you're right."

* * *

"I applied to be head chef at the Lucky, long, long ago," Amacy said, her eyes on the road ahead, not wanting to see the pity in Tristan's eyes. "She turned me down. Made me think I wasn't worthy of the job of chef. I've hated her for a while for that."

The streetlights flashed past them. When had it gotten dark?

The old hurt still ached, but now, with the presence of the wedding photos, it hurt worse. *If she knew me, why did she do that to me?*

"I haven't really thought about it, but that was ten years ago, right after I graduated from culinary school. She hasn't aged a day."

Hasn't aged a day. What if?

But no, that was impossible.

"I've started to wonder if she's not quite mortal," Tristan said. "I don't know much about leprechauns. But I'm pretty sure that the stories say that they're immortal. Or at least really long-lived. Stories of deals with great-grandfathers going on to follow the family for generations." he frowned, then added, "Now that I think of it, leprechauns usually aren't depicted as being good allies."

Amacy snorted. "I have a hard time thinking of her as an ally. Years can change a person. Especially if that person has to watch her friends die over and over again while she lives on. We should probably approach her as though she's not a friend."

Tristan's response was more impassioned than Amacy had expected. "Judge her by the actions we know instead of the actions of the past? Well, so far, she's given me a house and far too much money, so I don't know that I can judge her too harshly myself."

Amacy frowned and blushed at the same time. Maybe Fiona's current actions were frustrating, but she did seem to want good things for them. It was hard not to think about how she'd been treated ten years ago though.

They pulled up to the Lucky's parking lot without saying anything else and stopped at the hostess.

"We're not here to be seated," Amacy said. "We're here to see Fiona."

The hostess blinked, two menus in-hand, then shook her head. "Afraid that can't happen."

"No? Why not?" Amacy lashed her anger at the poor hostess.

Has she told her staff to refuse us entry?

"Fiona is out of town. She's not here."

Amacy deflated. "Any idea where she's gone?"

The girl shrugged. "Fiona and I aren't friends. She doesn't tell me that kind of stuff. And obviously, if she didn't tell you, you're not friends either. So. Maybe you should leave."

Very obviously not friends. To dump all this information onto them and then leave town without so much as a hint as to what they should do? Certainly not the type of thing a friend would do.

They left the restaurant and got back into her car. “Now what are we going to do?”

“Not much we can do, for the moment,” Tristan said. “Perhaps we can continue to search the house until Fiona comes back from wherever she’s gone? She can’t have anticipated being gone too long. She essentially told us to come by when we had questions. ‘You know where to find me,’ she said. Doesn’t sound like someone who’s going to traipse off and leave us behind, clueless.”

Amacy snorted. “You have far more faith in people than I do, I guess.”

Tristan gave her an amused smile. “Maybe I do.”

They drove back to the house, again in silence. Around them, the snow fell, muffling sound and spreading a fresh blanket on the quickly decaying surface of the old snow.

They walked into the kitchen and sat down at the table heavily, not even taking off their coats.

Tristan stared at the wood grain, and Amacy studied him. They were on their own, but not without their own resources. They had a way to get answers, but she wasn't sure if either of them was ready for more or not. Especially after what had happened last time. Her face heated as her libido reactivated at the memory of being pressed into Tristan's soft warm body.

Tristan looked up and said, "I'll be right back. I'm going to go get my laptop. Maybe some research will help us."

He got up and took off his coat, disappearing into the next room. Research would probably help, yes, but they had better methods than looking things up on the internet. Amacy waited while Tristan rummaged around.

He came back holding the laptop and its charging cord. “It’s dead,” he said, a look of chagrin coming across his face.

“Let it charge,” Amacy said. “There will be time for looking things up later.”

She held her hands out across the table and waited. Tristan set down the laptop on the table and plugged it in, sitting across from her. Outside, flurries swirled.

Tristan looked at Amacy’s outstretched hands as though they were snakes. Amacy tried hard not to take offense at that, certain Tristan didn’t know the look of disgust was open on his face.

Finally, Tristan sighed and reached out his own hands, laying them atop Amacy’s.

* * *

Will shakes rain off his hat as he hangs it next to the kitchen door, cradling something inside his coat under his right arm.

"What did you bring home this time?"

Will gives Alma a huge grin and pulls his coat away so she can see the large egg beneath. The surface is a burnished red, like a Fabergé egg.

Alma gasps, recognizing it instantly. "Where did you get that?"

Will frowns. He must see the fear on Alma's face. "I thought you'd be excited."

"There was a time and place for dragons, but they've been gone for thousands of years. Where did you get an egg?"

Will looks at the ceiling and puffs out his cheeks.

"You stole it," Alma says flatly. This wasn't the first time he'd seen something that reminded him of the past and just taken it.

"The owner didn't know what it was. And by the time he realizes it's gone, it won't exist anymore. Because we're going to hatch it."

Alma carefully sets down the dish she had been about to wash. "And why would we do that?"

Will looks hurt. "Chuck. We could bring him back. Be a whole group again, not just the four of us, but all five of us again. You know dragon souls can't reincarnate into anything but a dragon body. He was your best friend. I thought you would be happy."

Alma wipes her hands on the dish drying cloth. "But, Will, what if it's not him? What if we hatch this egg and it's someone else? Remember we used to fight dragons? Or what if it's a new soul, already destined to be born when it was formed? What then?"

* * *

Amacy never heard the answer, as she and Tristan resurfaced to the modern era.

Tristan stood up and filled up his electric kettle. “Tea?”

Amacy nodded, side-eyeing him. What had he said to convince her? Or had he done it without her? How complicit was Amacy in what happened?

Tristan clicked the kettle on and sat back down.

Amacy sighed. “This stuff doesn’t happen to normal people.”

They sat in silence for a few moments before a thought occurred to her. “What if Fiona didn’t mean for us to look for her at the Lucky but instead in Centralia? That’s where this dragon supposedly is trying to break free.”

Tristan raised his eyebrows. “That could be.”

“I have some days off back-to-back a few days from now. We could make a road trip out of it.”

Tristan didn’t seem to have any needs from his job beyond a wi-fi connection, which was everywhere from gas stations to restaurants to malls to parks nowadays. Amacy didn’t suspect he would have any objections. Not job-related anyway.

Tristan looked apprehensive but nodded anyway. “Okay.”

The kettle started bubbling and shut itself off, making them both jump.

Tristan got up and poured two cups, then said, “Would you like to go in the living room and watch the snow fall on the back yard?”

Amacy smiled. They’d never technically been on a date, not without being the third and fourth wheel to their own past. And this kind of time together seemed to be a perfect example of what life would be like, calm and unassuming.

If it weren't for that damned dragon, that was.

She finally took off her winter coat and hung it next to Tristan's. She took her tea into the living room and sitting next to Tristan on the couch, facing the glass doors looking out onto the small patio and the yard beyond.

They sat, not touching one another out of fear that they would trigger more memories when they wanted time just for them, drinking tea and watching the snow fall.

After a time, Tristan said in a low voice, "Do you see the fairies too?"

But it was just snow.

"Your eyes must be very sharp," Amacy said. "They're too small to see."

Tristan turned to look at her, and the look in his eyes nearly melted Amacy's insides to jelly. She'd never had anyone look at her like that before.

She took a sip of tea to keep herself from kissing Tristan right there. If a mere touch of hands brought on memories, what would a touch of lips do? They might never resurface. And though they had been together in a past life, it didn't mean that they could just pick up where their memories left off. In this life, she barely knew Tristan beyond that he was attractive and kind and all the things she'd ever looked for but never found in another person.

Tristan got up, and cranked up the old record player in the corner, and put the needle to the record. Amacy didn't know how to dance, but when Tristan held out his hand, she took it and was pulled into Tristan's body. Reality and history melded as she and Tristan danced along with the ghosts of Will and Alma to the same record in the same room, over a century apart.

Chapter 7

Pittsburgh, Pennsylvania, December 29

Tristan sat in his living room, laptop on his lap, a cup of tea in hand, not typing, not drinking. The night before, he and Amacy had parted not long after dancing together, the awkwardness setting in once again when the record was over. The intimacy of Will and Alma was jarring in the light of reality. He was left with the sensation that he was trying to impress a woman his family arranged a marriage with. They were strangers but still knew that they were meant to be together forever. And he could guess that chafed them both a little.

Neither one of them wanted to be with the other because they *had* to be. If they were going to be together, it was going to be because they *wanted* to be. And it was hard to come to terms with the fact he did.

To keep his mind off the conflicting thoughts, he surfed the internet, researching Pittsburgh around the 1900s. What he found disturbed him. The amount of mine fires around that time were very high. Had the dragon he had hatched in a past life killed all those people? Or was it, as it seemed, accidents? His stomach acid doubled capacity as he considered it. He took a sip of tea to settle it. Even if he was no longer Will, he couldn't help but feel responsible.

Would he feel compelled to hatch a dragon egg in this life? The visions notwithstanding, he had to admit he probably would. Just because he wouldn't believe that it was possible, but the part of him that did believe would never let him rest until he did. Thoughts of flying to work on a dragon were titillating. He didn't know anyone who wouldn't think having a pet dragon would be super awesome.

But then, he'd had the visions or memories or whatever they were. And he had seen that the reality did not match the fantasy.

He frowned as for the first time, he considered what exactly they could do to take care of a problem dragon. Obviously, they couldn't control it back then. And now it was bigger. He shuddered to think, so he got up and tried to find some other method of distracting himself.

As he walked around the house, he had the same sense that if he turned his head, someone else would be there. But, he was alone.

A sense of loss and absence clamped his gut. There weren't ghosts and that was almost more horrible than if there were. The house wasn't meant to hold one man alone.

To keep his mind off the situation, he decided to check the basement. If nothing else, perhaps there were a washer and dryer down there. He could certainly stand to wash his clothes. Maybe afterward, he would walk over to the clothing shop and buy something new. Ever since Amacy had come into his life, he had become increasingly aware of how bland his wardrobe, consisting of nothing but professional wear, was.

The door to the basement was next to the stairwell to the upstairs. He tried the handle and found the door locked. His hand reached up above the lintel as though of its own accord and pulled down a small silver key. Of course, it fit. He twisted the key, and the door opened easily. A string with a button tied to the end drew his attention up to a bare lightbulb. He pulled the string and the bulb glowed, showing the curling filaments of a past age inside.

The stairs were ancient, but sturdy. The wall was lined with shelves where old paint cans rusted, and as he descended, he discovered that there was storage to the back of each stair as well. Cans of beans and peas, far past their sell-by date sat dusty and unused in the area behind the foot tread. He thought it odd until he remembered that Will and Alma had lived through the depression. Like modern couponers, bulk was king.

He came to the bottom of the enclosed stairwell and was surprised to find that the basement carpeted. The wall to the right of the stairwell continued, the shadowy form of a door farther down. To the left, the space was large and open. Something flickered in the meager illumination of the naked bulb and he quickly flicked a switch along the right wall. Long overhead lights flickered on, their fluorescence sluggish.

Tristan laughed as an old, pitted mirror against the back wall refleted his own frightened face behind an ivory-painted bar. Old bottles sat on tiers in front of the glass, dusty stoppers rounded in the style of days past. The stools in front of the bar had now-cracked leather tops held on by brass tacks.

A few couches and small tables with chairs dotted the large open space. Pillars held up the ceiling, the floor of the kitchen and living room. It looked like a speakeasy. With another laugh, he realized that they would have been old enough in the '20s for that to possibly be exactly what it was. They'd apparently had lots of friends at one time or at least a clientele.

"What wild kids we were," he said with a laugh.

Curious, he turned his attention to the other room. He tried turning the knob, but like the door above, it was locked. He itched to find out what the other half held.

He let his mind wander as memory took over his body. He walked to a little cupboard under the stairs. Old moldering rag mops and toothless corn brooms stood inside, well used in their youth. A sink stood against the back wall, large and heavy. He turned to go and as he did, his eyes set upon the little hook deep under the instep of the stairs. A key, darkened by years and oxidization, hung from the hook.

He triumphantly took it down and went and unlocked the door. On the other side was a chemistry lab. A small window, milky with age, provided a source of both lighting and fresh air.

Right away, he felt at home. He took a deep breath and immediately regretted it as he started choking on the dust thickly laid over everything. In his past life, he had been a scientist. He'd never pursued science in this life since dangerous chemicals and hallucinations did not go hand-in-hand. He was gratified to know that he would have been successful if he'd tried.

He didn't know enough what kind of chemicals might be down here and what the ravages of time might have done to them, so he closed and locked the door once more, returning the key to its place. Likely, his old self's knowledge of chemistry had helped in his side-venture of thievery. A little thread of anguished embarrassment tickled him, and he decided he wouldn't think about that topic anymore.

He went over and inspected the bottles in the bar, wondering if they were still good. He suspected their unsealed tops wouldn't have done anything pleasant to them, but there was only one way to find out. No one would begrudge a man in his situation a drink or two.

He poured himself a glass of something unmarked and sniffed it. It had the sharp, painful tinge of alcohol to it. He took a sip and nearly spit it out, his eyes watering. It certainly hadn't gone bad. He swallowed it but decided perhaps the rest would do a better job as a household cleaner and poured it back in the bottle.

Still no washer and dryer. Perhaps in the last room upstairs.

He wandered back up the stairs from the basement and headed to the second floor.

Chapter 8

Pittsburgh, Pennsylvania, January 01

The second earthquake hit New Year's Day. Tristan was in the living room, reading his e-ARC when the couch became sentient and attempted to toss him to the floor. China jingled in the kitchen, and he wondered if he should run out and try to hold the cupboard shut to save it, but decided he would likely do more damage to himself in the scenario and he could always buy new dishes. So, he sat and waited, his e-reader still held upward as though he were still reading.

And then it was over. He sat still, uncertain. Nothing more happened. He set down his e-reader and picked up his phone. Maybe he should have gotten TV installed when he got the internet, but that would have meant that he would have had to get a TV. When the actors sometimes turned into strange things and slithered away, it tended to affect one's viewing habits, so he had never found it a necessary tool.

The headlines were there already, as they always would be in the digital age, preliminary headlines of "hey, an earthquake happened." Later, there would be more. His phone rang, covering over the sparse information the news provided.

Amacy.

He swiped to accept. "Hello."

"Hey, I'm driving over right now. My boss knows the pipes under my building broke last time. He thinks I'm leaving early to make sure my stuff is okay. But fuck my stuff, looks like we'd best figure this thing out before it's too late. It won't take me long to get there, so get ready to head to Centralia."

"As long as all the roads aren't on fire," Tristan quipped.

"Yeah, barring that."

He hung up and packed up all his stuff quickly. It helped that most of his worldly belongings still fit into his book bag.

Pennsylvania would never make an exciting travel destination. Tourism just wasn't in the books for a state filled with miles and miles of bare trees punctuated by snow-covered fields. There weren't many other people out and about on a cold New Year's Day after an earthquake. The only other vehicle they came across after the press of the city was a snowplow.

Tristan passed the time trying to read his book, though the rapidly changing brightness of the sun through the barren trees made that difficult. One moment, it was nearly too dark to read anything; the next, the sun was a laser-beam. At times, the light took on a strobe-like flicker. He was quickly nauseated and put down the book, which really didn't change the situation with his stomach any.

They rode in silence, each wrapped in their own personal cloud of thoughts they did not feel like sharing with the other.

Four hours of nothing ate away at the day. By the time signs for Centralia started popping up along the highway, the sky had gone dark. And the word "highway" was probably an over-dramatization of the two-lane they drove down. Ahead, through the density of empty tree branches, a light signaled some kind of civilization. A gas station materialized to their right, lights blazing, lot empty.

They pulled in, and Amacy spoke for the first time since leaving Pittsburgh. “Maybe the attendant knows of some place we can bed down for the night and start our search again in the morning.”

“Good plan.” Tristan unfolded himself, as usual unhappy with the fact that cars were generally designed for the “average” height group.

The cold of the air outside the car drove Tristan after Amacy faster than he normally would have walked.

Inside, a woman with bleach-blonde hair and a bored stare flicked her gaze to them. “What can I do for you folks?”

Her demeanor changed at the sight of them, a smile pulling her pink-lipsticked lips from their frown, a born saleswoman.

Amacy approached the counter. “We’re looking for a place to stay the night nearby.”

The woman, Doreen as her nametag said, shook her head. "That's going to be a little difficult. After that second quake today, scientists and journalists have swarmed the place. Pretty sure all the motels are full-up. You can always try, I suppose," she said, writing down names of hotels and directions on the back of a take-out menu featuring typical gas station fare such as hot dogs and salmonella sandwiches.

"Thanks," Amacy said, and turned to leave, but Doreen's voice stopped her.

"Oh. If none of those have a place for you, you could always try that Mexican guy's B and B. He might take you two since he's been refusing all the others. Bad business move, if you ask me. Come here, and I'll write the directions for that too."

Doreen scrawled further instructions to the bed and breakfast, then, before handing it back, she said, "Now if you two are here to try to get a look at Centralia, know that the cops aren't turning a kind eye on thrill-seekers. Not with all the others already clamoring for their space there. Isn't safe for anyone, let alone a pair of young things like you."

"Just passing through," said Amacy, and Doreen nodded, satisfied.

She relinquished the paper and said, "Maybe come back when it's nicer and you can marvel then."

They escaped the gas station.

Back in the car, Amacy clicked on the overhead light and looked at the hastily scrawled instructions. "Well, most of these are nearby. We can check them out, then if that doesn't work, try that ominous-sounding, not at all murdery bed and breakfast."

As Doreen had predicted, all the tiny hotels and motels in the area were full-up.

Just their luck.

They drove toward a large farmhouse down a road one click above a dirt path. Empty fields stood on either side, watching their progress. Lights were still on in the house, a good sign.

Amacy pulled her car into a cubby of less snow next to a robin's egg blue Mini Cooper. She eyed the rust pitting the lower part of the car with a mixture of sadness and disgust. To treat a beautiful piece of classic machinery with such disrespect felt like sacrilege. She patted the hood of her well-maintained vehicle to reassure it she would never allow the same to happen to it. They trudged past the sad little Mini in ankle-high snow. No one had been out to maintain in a while, it seemed.

The stairs were a better, having been brushed recently. Amacy pressed a lighted doorbell next to the door and waited. Behind her, Tristan rubbed his arms and stamped his feet a little. Amacy had to smile. The guy just didn't seem to be able to take the cold. She wondered how Tristan had survived farther north in Chicago before she decided he probably just never left the house.

She reached out an arm and wrapped it around Tristan's middle, offering a little of her own heat. Tristan froze in place, and Amacy forced herself not to pull away, chastened. After what Tristan had told her of his life, he had likely not had much in the way of physical affection, which made Amacy's soul hurt a little. Everyone needed someone to hold them from time to time.

The door opened inward swiftly, the movement nearly pulling her into the room with its force. A giant man stood there, tall and burly, black hair trailing down past his shoulders. He looked like some ancient Aztec god. She half-expected him to be wearing a jaguar pelt from his shoulders.

“Yes?” His accent was subtle, but he still sounded a little like Antonio Banderas.

Suddenly feeling vulnerable, wondering if this was actually the right place, Amacy said, “We heard that you run a bed and breakfast? We’re looking for somewhere to stay for the night.”

“Oh, that,” he said. “I do. Please come in.”

His response sounded strange, but Amacy was cold and tired and hungry, so she rolled with it.

He stood back, and they came into the house on an entry hall, a desk tucked next to the stairwell, a large ledger-like book open on its top. Little cubbies climbed up the wall behind the desk like old-fashioned mail slots from hotels in black and white movies. Her nerves settled at the sight. It was a bed and breakfast after all. She tried not to think of Alfred Hitchcock as she continued her inspection.

The house smelled of cinnamon, and through the archway to the right, she could see a Christmas tree still set up in the living room. Through the archway to the left, a large dining room table was set with a single plate and cup. Along the ceiling, large old-fashioned Christmas lights lined the crown molding. Even if the host was a little overwhelming, the place was clean and pleasant and well-presented.

The man walked over to the desk, and Tristan pulled the door closed behind them.

“Welcome, welcome,” the man rumbled as he flipped through some pages in the large book. “You have the pick of the rooms. There is a room with a queen bed, one with twin bunks, and two rooms with single twin beds. What would you prefer?”

He looked up, pen in hand, waiting for their reply. Suddenly blushing, Amacy glanced over at Tristan. Her companion had his lips pressed together in an awkward expression, obviously not wanting to speak his mind.

“The room with the queen,” Amacy said, feeling bold.

The big man smiled and jotted something in the ledger. Setting the pen in the spine, he said, “Would you like some dinner? I have some chili on the stove.”

Tristan, having been silent just a moment ago, nearly leapt across Amacy to accept time spent outside the single-bed room.

She kept herself from rolling her eyes. Guy didn’t know what he wanted, and it wasn’t her fault. With a sudden thought, she side-eyed the tall man, wondering if he had survived to his thirties a virgin.

Their host brought them into the dining room and motioned for them to sit. “My name is Shrew,” he said. “Please make my home your home.”

He left, and Amacy leaned over the table and whispered, “What kind of name is Shrew?”

Tristan shrugged, his face pale.

Amacy's eyes lighted upon a small pot with a little green plant growing from it, a grow-light above it. It sat in the corner like a family heirloom or trophy, lighted for attention.

She had been so mesmerized by it that she didn't notice Shrew's return until he slid a bowl of chili and a napkin full of flatware in front of her.

Amacy pointed to the weirdly hypnotic plant. "What's that?"

Shrew frowned and turned his face away from her for a moment as though he did not want her to see his expression. He set Tristan's chili in front of him before responding. "I'm a potato farmer. That's my seed potato."

Amacy frowned. She didn't know much about potato farming, but keeping a seed potato inside didn't seem quite right. She was pretty sure freezing was an important step of creating a seed potato, but the spicy scent of the chili before her drew any further thought of the plant from her head. It was delicious from the first spoonful to the last, leaving her with that pleasant sense of euphoric torpor that usually follows consuming hot, spicy food. She would have to recommend this place to her painfully single friend, Jenna. She could use a man who could cook in her life.

Tristan wished he would have asked for an alcoholic beverage with dinner as Shrew led them up the stairs to their shared bedroom. The house was pleasant enough. Not too cold, even though old farmhouses tended toward drafty.

But he was being led upstairs to a double bed with a woman who, when they touched, he was sent back in time. And though Amacy didn't seem to notice, the man leading them to their bed had been there. In the past.

The man on the stairs ahead of them was the man from the photo album. And after thinking about it hard enough, Tristan had realized that he was also the man who had flickered into and out of existence at the bus station in Chicago. Tristan had to wonder if the small woman with her hood up had been Fiona.

“Here’s your room,” Shrew rumbled and opened the door, flipping the light switch. The room inside was homey and pleasant, not at all frightening.

It did not stop his anxiety though. They were obviously on the right track, but for whatever reason, the big man was playing the host, not hinting at his possible creepy immortality and their connection to him.

“The bathroom is down the hall.” Shrew pointed to a small, open door. “Feel free to freshen up. There are towels on the dresser. If you so desire, you may join me after in the living room. I’ve been completely hooked on *Downton Abbey* lately, and I've been binge-watching all the episodes."

He gave them a smile then shuffled away down the stairs.

Tristan pulled Amacy into the room and shut the door. Amacy laid a surprised glance to where Tristan's hand grasped her arm, and Tristan dropped it immediately. He'd obviously not thought of the consequences.

Amacy asked, "Why didn't we fall into a memory?"

Relief washed over Tristan. "No bare skin," he guessed. "But don't you recognize him?"

Amacy shook her head. "Should I?"

Tristan had spent more time looking at the photos than Amacy had. "That guy's in the photo album I found. He and Fiona are in almost every picture together."

Amacy turned pale. "Why didn't you say something?"

"When could I have said something? I'm not going to bring it up right in front of him. 'Oh, by the way, you haven't aged a day since 1905?'"

Amacy shrugged. "Geez. Well, we could have asked him what was going on instead of going through a charade of just passing through."

She was angry, but Tristan couldn't figure out why. Had he made her feel like a fool? That was usually why people got angry. It didn't matter. He didn't need to know why to apologize.

"I'm sorry," he said. "I just wasn't sure what to do and froze up. I didn't know you didn't recognize him, and I was following your lead."

Amacy's feathers unruffled, and she sat down on the bed. "Well, we could either go down and talk or we could explore more memories. What would you like to do?"

Tristan got the feeling that Amacy was offering more than just memories, but the idea of sex made him nervous. He certainly wanted Amacy that way, but he overanalyzed things like that sometimes and he was afraid he would be an unsatisfactory lover. If they were meant to be together forever and he couldn't satisfy her sexually, where would they be?

Amacy sighed. "Well, you are clearly not the one to make decisions here. You freeze up like a popsicle. I'm not after sex. Not yet."

Amacy got up and walked across the room, pushing her arms under Tristan's and around his torso. She leaned her head forward onto Tristan's upper chest.

Without much thought about it, Tristan wrapped his arms around Amacy's body as well. She was warm and fit nicely against Tristan's chest. His heart sped up as he inhaled the coconut scent of Amacy's hair. But nothing happened. No vision of the past.

Amacy pulled back and reached up to the collar of Tristan's shirt and began unbuttoning buttons. Panicked, Tristan pulled back and Amacy smiled. "Skin-to-skin contact. I'm not going to force you into anything you're not ready for. You can trust me."

When Amacy reached for the buttons again, Tristan allowed her. Amacy unbuttoned the shirt to mid-sternum and pulled two halves apart, then put her arms round him again and when the side of her face touched bare clavicle, the room disappeared.

Chaos. Screams. Blood.

Chapter 9

Pittsburgh, Pennsylvania, 1908

Will and Alma sneak down the alleyway, each grasping a handle of the large wicker basket they carry between them. Inside is a pile of old sheets and a burnished-penny-red dragon egg. Blankets are thrown over top the egg to hide it and keep it warm. If anyone sees them, they'll assume that they're out to do their laundry.

At two in the morning.

They hurry through the streets of Pittsburgh, the steam and glow of the steel mills guiding them to their ultimate goal.

As they near, the orange glow flickering ahead, the heat palpable, Alma's steps slow. "Are you sure?"

She has to ask one last time, before what they plan to do changes their lives forever.

Ash falls from the sky above them, dancing around them like snow flurries. The fires dance their own demonic dance in the shadows and across Will's face.

"No," Will says at last. "But if we don't, it could die. Doesn't it deserve a chance at life?"

Alma can't be certain.

"Wouldn't you love to have Chuck back? Like old times?"

Alma frowns. Why does he have to keep throwing that back in her face? She loved Chelinathnos, Chuck, like a brother. He had been her best friend. But that had been so many lives ago. And in every life since, she has mourned him and come to terms with the loss.

It isn't fair that Will can pull her in to something so foolhardy by tweaking the exact right heartstring. Every time.

She sighs and grasps the handle of the basket, lifting it once more.

They continue on.

Alma stands in the kitchen with a tiny red dragon the size of a small lizard. The house has been much warmer since he came into their lives, and she stands in her shirtsleeves and petticoat. He looks at her expectantly and she smiles down at him. "Go ahead and light it, Brasmanathnon," she says. He rears up on his back legs and blows flames into the fire box on the stove.

"Good boy," Alma shouts, clapping her hands. Brasmanathnon jumps up and down in happiness as well.

* * *

Alma bats frantically at the curtains, aflame and threatening to catch the rest of the house on fire. Brasmanathnon sits on his haunches behind her, whining. He just doesn't seem capable of the human-like intelligence Chuck was. Is it his age? She isn't sure. But either way, he is too big and too dangerous to keep in the house. What if he gets into the basement and blows fire at Will's chemistry items? He could kill them all.

Will comes home just as the last of the flames had been dampened. As usual, Brasmanathnon meets him like a puppy at the door and Will responds in kind. Not the way a parent greets a child, though that may be more of a defense mechanism than anything else. They could never have a child of their own. It is easy most days to tell herself that it's a blessing. They'd sacrificed ever having children when they'd joined their souls. No sense linking another soul to their endless roll of the wheel of lives. But other days, her heart aches with the desire to be a mother.

Will comes into the living room, scratching Brasmanathnon between the ears. Alma knows she looks a mess, in her shirtsleeves in the living room covered in ash. Will comes over and kisses her then wraps her in a hug. "I'm sorry," he says into Alma's ear. "I thought this would be better."

The sadness Alma feels breaks free, and she weeps on Will's shoulder. "What should we do?"

Will pulls her to the sofa and settles her upon it before opening the door off the living room and letting Brasmanathnon out into their fenced back yard. He returns to Alma and takes her hands. "It's almost winter. He's well trained, and he knows we love him. We bring him to a cave in the woods, and he'll do what dragons do in the winter—hibernate."

Alma frowns. "He's never hibernated here."

"That's because we keep the house warm."

Alma looks down at her hands. "Will he hate us? I don't know how much he understands. If we leave him...." She can't make herself go on. He might become everything they feared. But they can't keep him at the house anymore.

And the only other option is too awful to stomach. They brought him to life; he deserved to live it out. She nodded.

The next day, Brasmanathnon is gone, and Alma's heart is filled with anxiety, both for their little dragon and for whether or not they made the right decision.

As the winter wears on, so do the incidences of mine fires. They read about them in the newspaper, but all the fires are explained easily. Open flames. Pockets of gas. But deep in her belly, Alma wonders.

When they go back in the spring, Brasmanathnon is not where they left him and there is no sign he had ever been there at all.

All those deaths. There is only one explanation. But there is no way to find him. How does one find a runaway dragon with the intelligence of a Labrador retriever?

Chapter 10

Centralia, Pennsylvania, January 01

Tristan and Amacy broke apart. Amacy saw the man before her with new eyes. In the past, he had been selfish and undisciplined. How much of personality transferred from life to life? How much of that was hidden beneath the amiable exterior Tristan displayed? Suddenly cold and unimaginably sad, Amacy put her arms around herself and rubbed them for warmth. A man like that was not a man she wanted to spend any more lives with, history or no. She'd dated women and men both who took her for granted, and hell if she was going to waste another life on a person like that.

* * *

Tristan shuddered. Something had been wrong, very wrong with his vision. He felt as though he was coated in oil. His entire vision had been spent in some strange feeling of trance somewhere between waking and dreaming. He hadn't made decisions on his own. Something else had been guiding him. It left a coppery taste in his mouth, like that of blood. But there was no blood.

"I'll sleep on the loveseat," he said, and Amacy did not argue. He wished he knew what Amacy had seen. Had she seen those moments, deep inside, when Past Him had desired power more than love? Did Amacy think he was the same person? It was hard to disprove. But still, the not-rightness remained, like looking at the world through a dirty window.

He lay down, anxiety biting him. He had caused this, but he couldn't figure out why. Something had been wrong with Will, and he wanted to know what in order to make sure it wasn't still wrong. Could something infect a soul, not just a mind?

It was *his* fault all those poor miners had died. He should have done something from the beginning, the right thing while the dragon was still small. Before he had shown his true colors to the world.

Bile in his throat, Tristan stared at the ceiling, wondering if he should apologize for his past self. He glanced over and saw Amacy had laid down and rolled to face away. She was obviously angry, but that made no sense. That man he'd been...that wasn't him anymore.

He was someone else, and whatever had been wrong with Will was already fading from his consciousness. That wasn't him. It wasn't his fault. But still, he would be expected to fix it. And fix it he would try to do, to hold on to the one thing in his life that truly mattered. If she ever really was his to hold in the first place.

Chapter 11

Centralia, Pennsylvania, January 02

Eventually, the sun rose, and Tristan felt it was probably acceptable to go downstairs. He got up off the love seat, and his back crackled. There was a time when his body could have handled sleeping in a love seat, but that had ended somewhere around his thirtieth birthday.

Amacy was still asleep, or at least miming admirably. Tristan closed the door behind him with barely a click. Without consciously deciding to, he remained quiet down the hallway and down the first half of the stairs.

Voices drifted up to him. Another traveler must have arrived in the night. But something in the tenor of the voice made him crouch down on the step and listen harder.

"Maybe this time, we can fix this," said a familiar voice. "He doesn't seem as hard-headed as last time."

Fiona. The visitor was Fiona. Tristan sighed.

"Maybe this time we can talk some sense into him." Fiona's voice held more than a trace of long-suffering airs.

They're talking about me.

Might as well join the conversation if he was to be the topic. He walked the rest of the way down the stairs and found Shrew and Fiona sitting at the dining room table, drinking tea.

"We just can't seem to go anywhere without bumping into you," Tristan said.

Fiona laughed. "No, you really can't. Come on, sit down. Shrew, get some tea."

Shrew got up from the table, and Tristan sat down.

"Seeing as how you and your lady love spent the night together last night, perhaps we can finally have a rational conversation about this," Fiona said as Shrew set a cup of steaming black tea in front of Tristan.

Tristan blushed and shook his head, more in disbelief than negating that he and Amacy had spent the night together. "I still don't see how you both fit into this."

Fiona smiled and reached out a small hand, setting it over Tristan's. A stream of past lives washed over him, and in every memory, Shrew and Fiona were by his side. The quickness and insubstantiality of the memories left him feeling a little nauseated, and when Fiona took her hand away, he took a sip of her tea to calm his roiling stomach.

“You could say we’re BFFs,” Fiona said.

“But you never change,” Tristan said before he could stop himself.

“Sure, we do. Everyone changes. But you’re right, we are a little more permanent than the average person. Shrew and I are immortal. You already know what I am, a leprechaun.”

Fiona quieted and looked over at Shrew, who took a deep sip of his tea to avoid saying anything. She sighed. “Shrew is a potato sprite. As long as his potato or any of its descendants lives, so does he.”

Tristan tried not to show surprise on his face. He’d never heard of a potato sprite before. Tree, yes, potato no.

“It’s a perfectly viable plant,” Shrew said, his voice quiet and defensive. “I’ve lived on while others have lost their lives in deforestation.”

In an attempt to comfort the obviously defensive sprite, Tristan supplied the only thing he knew about the root vegetable. “Potatoes originated in the Andes didn’t they?”

Shrew beamed at him over his tea mug. “Yes, they did. I appreciate your not laughing. Amacy’s soul always laughs at me. I like this version of you since you didn’t laugh. That is my plant in the corner. I am big and strong because it is robust. It is much easier to keep it so these days.”

“What are we keeping robust?” Amacy had arrived in the doorway. “Oh,” she added when her gaze took in Fiona at the table as well.

“Sit down, dear one,” Fiona said, “We have enough time to explain it all over again.”

* * *

Fiona broke the silence. “We need to assess the situation, see how much time we have. Two earthquakes in a week makes it seem like maybe we don't have a lot."

Shrew nodded, solemn. "I will drive."

Amacy held out a hand. "We can't just break in. Doreen said there were cops to keep people out. And the smoke is toxic."

"Oh, no, *the smoke is toxic*," Fiona said in a mocking voice. "Better stay away and let the feckin' dragon break through and kill everyone."

Amacy frowned. "That's not what I meant."

"That'n is a meanie sometime," said Shrew in a rumbling voice. His six-foot-seven frame, muscular as they came, seemed so incongruous with his words. And his plant affinity.

Amacy held back a snicker at the thought of a potato sprite.

"Let me ask you this," Shrew said. "Have you ever seen a sprite before?"

Amacy shrugged, trying to act as though she didn't feel like he'd just read her mind. "Would I know if I had?"

"You've not seen a sprite before other than me because I want you to see me. Sprites survive because they can make others not see them. And we can extend that ability to those around us. It's really helpful."

"That's how you kept out of my sight at the bus station," Tristan said. "You drifted in and out of my sight."

That was new to Amacy.

Shrew blushed. "You are too good with your eyes. You could always see the things others would ignore or things others would rather keep hidden."

"Do I have to pick you guys up and put you in the car myself?" Fiona got up and cleared away the teacups. "Get going. I'll do some laundry. Wash the sheets off your bed on hot, dear ones."

She gave Tristan and Amacy an impish grin then disappeared into the kitchen.

“We had best go then,” Shrew said, “Fiona has spoken.” He sounded so serious, but he ended his statement with a laugh.

They all put on their winter gear and shuffled out to the blue Mini.

“I bought this when I was shorter,” he said apologetically, glancing at Tristan, who was nearly as tall.

They all climbed in, Shrew and Tristan taking a few moments to readjust the seats in the front as Amacy waited patiently in the back. Though she wasn’t short, she never had the same trouble as others when it came to small spaces. Give her enough room to put her legs in, and she was fine. After some further fiddling, they buckled up started out.

Shrew turned on the radio, cycling through the stations until he found one he liked.

Amacy tried not to laugh as they listened to ‘80s soft rock the few miles of back roads they drove to the town of Centralia. They parked around a bend in the road, the other end invisible. “There’s a police blockade around the corner,” Shrew said. “Now, as long as you are quiet, they should not notice you. Don’t speak. Walk quietly.”

“We’re just going to walk past the cops?” Amacy still didn’t quite believe his power.

“That is the idea. The car would make too much noise. They would see us.”

Amacy shook her head but got out of the car.

The three of them walked along the road, Shrew first, Amacy behind him, Tristan trailing along at the back.

A pair of young cops sat in the cruiser parked next to the sawhorse across the road. One was eating a sandwich, the other staring out the window, seemingly directly at them.

Amacy swallowed hard and tried not to notice. She looked directly at the back of Shrew's head. He walked on by the police car, and the officer continued to stare up the road the way they'd come. On the other side of the sawhorse, they kept walking until they came to a curve in the road and their first look at the town shrouded in mist and smoke.

Snow crunched beneath their feet, and though they were far out of the line of sight of the police officers, they remained silent. The air was smoky and hazy, the road beneath their feet cracked.

"What happened here? Surely, not all of this was caused by the earthquake," Amacy said, finally breaking the silence.

"No," said Shrew, waving his hand ahead of them. The air cooled and cleared of smoke for a few feet. "In 1962, a garbage fire went down into the mine. Burned and burned. Brasmanathnon did the rest. But he's too big to get out now."

"I don't understand."

"He's been here for years. Possibly since he abandoned the mines around Pittsburgh. Nothing nicer for a dragon than to be near a coal mine. They eat the stuff."

Amacy quieted again. She'd never considered what dragons ate. She'd always assumed meat.

But the eerie lack of bird song or nearby cars or anything else got to her and she had to talk again. "How long have you and Fiona known he was here?"

"Some time now. Before Will and Alma became Tristan and Amacy. But then, you were too old to do anything about it, so we kept silent. We waited as long as we could to give you as normal a life as possible this time. Even though we knew we would have to get you sooner or later. I suppose sentimentality kept us from wakening you to the hidden world where we exist before now."

Amacy was going to ask more, like how they always knew where she and Tristan were despite their different bodies, but Shrew held out a hand and held them back. It took Amacy a moment to realize they were no longer the only sound in the trees. Up ahead, a group of people chattered.

"It is time for silence again," Shrew said. "No matter what you see, stay silent or they will see you."

They broke out across the snowy ground, up a hill, and through the trees. At the top, they discovered all the journalists, gathered around the remains of the church. It was split down the center, each side still standing above a flaming maw below.

The journalists spoke loudly over one another to their news stations. Amacy doubted if they would even notice if she and her companions made a sound. She stood in awe of it. She had seen it on television days before, but the heat of the flames had melted the snow around the building and threatened to singe the brows off her face.

In that moment, it all became real. This was a problem that she was meant to fix. And it was so huge and beyond her that she was utterly immobilized.

Shrew's hand gripped her arm, encased in a thick layer of winter coat, and pulled her away.

They tromped back to the car in complete silence. No one needed a reminder to remain quiet as they passed the police officers.

In the car, Shrew said, "Now you see why it is so important to reawaken the powers we know you have. Your magic and Tristan's skill in the arts of war. We need you both in top shape."

A little of Amacy's fog of fear blew away as Shrew turned on the car. "Magic?"

"Absolutely. You have the soul of an elf. You have magic and always will. All you need to do is wake it up."

Wake it up. Like a sleeping puppy.

Tristan sat wooden in the front seat, stone-struck. His emotions were too many to choose just one, though fear was trying its hardest to be the top dog.

This is my fault.

Scientifically, earthquakes did not cause giant rents in the earth. It just didn't happen. So that rent, that huge, deep maw...that was his fault.

"Were there any people in the church? When it happened?" he could barely hear his own voice over the '80s soft rock. He couldn't expect anyone else to. Maybe it was for the best. Maybe he didn't want to hear the answer.

"Very few people visit churches in the middle of the night, Tristan," Shrew said.

Oh. *Oh.* Thank goodness.

Tristan relaxed. "All the townspeople?"

"They have survived and been relocated. There were not many residents left."

So, no one had died. Not yet anyway.

He slumped in his seat. It was too much. Finding a woman who might have loved him without the intrusive memories was not sufficient tradeoff. His unprincipled past self had ruined love for his current self.

His situation was hard enough without having to try to make up for who he couldn't remember being. Without a huge god-damned dragon that same awful man had lost. He could go back in time and throttle himself. It turned out it his mother was right. He was a screw-up and had been for many lives.

* * *

Amacy sat through Tristan's questions, quiet, attentive. She wondered how much of this they could have avoided if she would have just stood up to Will back then. What had been wrong with her that she couldn't say no to an obviously foolhardy idea? Was it fear that if she said something that their perfect, foretold marriage would be over? They couldn't have been much older than 18 before they had gotten married. Who knew what the marriage pool was like in the 1900s for a black woman in Pittsburgh?

This wasn't turning out the way she wanted to at all. She'd always wanted to meet the man from her dreams. But she hadn't realized that when she did, she would find that their last life had been spent together in a bad marriage and had started a disaster.

She was frustrated and lost. And for the first time, she considered that maybe Tristan was too. She wasn't the same girl who went along with whatever her spouse said, so it stood to reason that Tristan wasn't the same kind of jerk who expected it. Maybe he was exactly what he had presented to the world, a shy and caring guy with his own insecurities.

She reached out a hand and touched Tristan's shoulder.

How can I be angry? He's already beating himself up enough for the both of us. For something he wasn't even alive for.

Tristan reached up and touched Amacy's wrist, making sure to not touch bare skin so that they didn't get transported back into their last life. But then, he let it drop again and went back to staring out the window.

Feeling awkward, Amacy drew her hand back again and leaned against her chair once more.

“There is no fight in him this life is there?” Shrew asked the question, quiet and concerned.

“It does not seem that way,” Amacy agreed, wondering if somehow their natures had swapped. She felt as though in the face of ten men, she would fight them to the death as long as she could protect those she loved.

Fiona met them at the door. She took their coats and helped Tristan to the couch in the living room as though he were an invalid. And in some ways, he felt as though he was.

“I’ve made hot chocolate,” she said. “I’ll go get it off the stove. Shrew, come help carry the cups?”

Shrew lumbered off to the kitchen behind the tiny, sprightly Fiona, and Amacy sat down at the other end of the couch. “We made a mess last life, didn’t we?”

Tristan couldn't bring himself to reply. Part of him thought maybe he was overreacting, but it turned out that he was the little sheltered child his mother had brought him up to be after all. After her death, Tristan was the one who kept himself from negative feelings. He had no idea how to deal with failure head-on.

He had to stop hiding. For the good of the world. And that was terrifying.

"What are we going to do?" he asked through numb lips.

Amacy leaned across the space between them, putting a hand on Tristan's knee. "First, we are going to listen to what these two have to say. I don't think we can do this on our own. And I think we've seen today that magic is real. There is no way a pack of journalists like that would have left us alone, walking out of the woods like that, if Shrew's magic wasn't real. And no way the cops would have let us enter and exit untouched."

Tristan put his face in his hands. "Unfortunately, that's part of what I find distressing. Until today, when we went there, I could pretend this wasn't real. That we were just having a silly adventure and at the end of it, I would go back to my house and money that I had no right to, and we would live our lives.

"But seeing what we saw today... Earthquakes can't do what happened to the church. I can't pretend that nothing is going on here. And that frightens me to no end because that means that I have to fight a dragon. A dragon that I know we both loved before. And a dragon whom I'm pretty sure did something to me."

Amacy opened her mouth to speak, but at that moment, Shrew came into the room with a tray of mugs, and following directly behind him was Fiona, carrying a sword just as tall as she was. Why they hadn't come in with the opposite items was beyond Tristan, but before he could stop himself, he began to laugh. Next to him, Amacy caught his eye and smiled as well.

“Shut up,” Fiona said, succinctly. And that was enough to make it so.

Shrew handed Amacy a mug and set Tristan’s on a coaster on the side-table next to him.

Fiona approached and held out the sword. He’d never imagined holding a sword, but just like when he’d first met Amacy, his heart filled with the feeling of seeing someone he knew and loved and missed. He reached out and took the hilt. It was like touching ice and then fire. His palm tingled. And then the room around him was gone.

So many images. They all blurred together. Fiona, Amacy, Shrew, and an array of fantastic creatures only ever seen in books or movies flashed past, faces changing, the group expanding and contracting as friends came and left. And blood, but never blood in anger and hate, but blood to protect, blood to save.

A rightness came over him, and suddenly, he knew that all those things that he had seen that her mother had called hallucinations had actually been him seeing the world as it was—full of wonder and the fantastic that most people never noticed.

His arms held a strength he'd never imagined possible. His body felt vigorous and whole and well.

He was hungry.

For life. For what was right. For love.

He looked up at Amacy, and all her faces from over the years hazed around the edges of her own face then melded together, and he realized all the faces she'd ever worn were clearly visible in the one she wore now. He knew her, inside out, heart, soul. Their essences were mated to one another, entwined for eternity. He would do anything for her, for the knowledge that he would spend the rest of their lives together as well. He leaned the sword against the arm of the couch to go to her and....

It was all gone.

He was just Tristan again. It was disconcerting, as though he had been himself for the first time in his life for a few seconds but no longer.

"How do we make the effect permanent?"

* * *

Amacy was having trouble catching her breath. That look Tristan had given her had sent chills up and down her spine. She was still trembling.

The intensity of it felt like he had seen directly into her, understanding her and accepting her. It was the single most intimate thing that she'd ever experienced in her life. She'd read novels with characters who stared dreamily into one another's eyes for hours. She'd always thought it overdramatic, but in that moment, all she wanted to do was continue to look into Tristan's eyes.

"How do we make the effect permanent?"

Tristan's question was met with Shrew plunking himself down between them on the couch and saying, "It cannot be permanent, but you can get a sense of permanency with practice. Understanding it will control the memories so that your flesh can touch someone else's without being overwhelmed with them."

Fiona came to the side of the couch and said to Amacy, "Let's leave these two to talk about swords and fighting. I think some fresh air and a walk in the woods will help clear our heads. It's been a crazy day."

Amacy still wasn't sure how to feel about Fiona after her grand betrayal years ago, but she knew a "we need to get out of their hair for a bit" when she heard one.

She got up and followed Fiona to the kitchen, taking as deep of sips of her hot chocolate as she could before she had to abandon it. Hot chocolate never reheated well.

"Can't we just give them space in the kitchen?" She wanted to be warm, not to crunch around in snow. She'd done that already that day.

"We need to start your training as well. And you've always been at your best in nature."

"That's the elf in me, right?"

Fiona laughed. "Shrew's been talking, hasn't he? He always likes to talk to people about their natures. Did you know that elves aren't gone?"

They set their mugs on the counter. "What do you mean? I've never seen an elf."

Fiona drew her into the hallway, where a mirror hung on the wall. “Elves were lucky. They passed enough for human that they weren’t all caught right away.”

Fiona turned her to face the mirror. “They interbred with humans. You’re about two-thirds elf, genetically.”

That said, Fiona reached up and pulled Amacy’s hair back from her ear and the tiniest brush of Fiona’s hand on her ear brought a rush of memories. Talking. Laughing. Drinking together. Laying in the grass and watching clouds. They had been the best of friends. At one time.

Whatever Fiona had been telling her was lost in the memories and the deepening of the betrayal. “Why didn’t you hire me?” She blurted it out, unable to hold it in.

Fiona jerked visibly in the mirror and stepped back. She looked pale, guilty. “I’d hoped you’d forgotten that.”

“How could I forget it? You insulted me. My cooking.” She whirled to face Fiona.

Fiona looked so childlike, looking down at her clasped hands. "I wanted you to have a normal life. Sometimes, Shrew and I are so glad to have you back that we push you back into it too soon. We decided that was what we'd done wrong last time. We didn't want to get it wrong again this time."

Amacy remained silent as she digested what Fiona said.

"You saw what happened with an accidental touch. I needed to keep you away and make sure you didn't come back looking for a job again. Something like that in a kitchen would be dangerous both to you and the rest of my staff. I couldn't risk you to a stupid mistake."

Amacy shook her head. "But god damn it, you messed me up. I haven't tried for a chef job since. I've been working as a cashier at a sandwich shop."

Fiona looked up at Amacy, the color in her green leprechaun eyes swirling in a way

Amacy now recognized as how Fiona looked when she was sad. “I didn’t mean to. I misjudged. It was meant to encourage you, to desire to prove me wrong, not to internalize and accept. I apologize for that. It is always difficult to know how much of your attributes will come to the forefront every life. I think because you look so much like your last you, I goaded in a way I knew would work for the last her.”

Fiona stopped, looking confused. “Referring to your past selves becomes confusing sometimes. If only you and he could be immortal like Shrew and I. You could have been. But you chose long ago that if he died, you died. And you tied yourself to him forever. Most god-damned beautiful thing I’ve ever experienced.”

Amacy laughed, all the internalized pain and hatred opening itself and dissipating as though it never had been. “Thank you for letting me live my life rather than Alma’s again.”

Fiona smiled. “I’d hoped you would be able to see it that way.”

Amacy leaned down and wrapped her arms around the smaller woman. “Thank you for being my friend through everything. Every girl needs a friend she knows she can trust to do the right thing, even if it’s painful.”

“Yeah, yeah,” Fiona said, her brogue deepening as she tried to push Amacy away. “Enough hugging. Let’s go get our coats.”

It wasn’t as cold outside as she remembered it. Shrew’s yard was nice, if small. Most of the land was around the sides, where his fields lay under snow. Behind the couple feet of snow-covered lawn was a forest. Fiona maneuvered them toward this. Once inside the trees, an even deeper calm descended upon

Amacy, and she wondered how she could have lived her entire life in the city.

Her soul lived in outdoor spaces.

Fiona led her through the woods to a small cement gazebo. They sat down together on the cold stone benches. They sat and listened to the twittering winter birds and scufflings in the snow from small mammals. Somewhere farther on there was a stream. She could hear it tumbling over itself in the background. But other than that, nothing.

No cars, no people.

And despite the anxiety earlier, being so close to nature filled her with a calm power. She could almost feel the forest wrapping her deep within itself.

"I was going to attack you when we came out here," Fiona said, quiet, surprising Amacy out of her quiet contemplation.

"What?" She was too shocked to truly comprehend.

"In the past, that's what has brought your powers back quickest, being in danger. But I couldn't do that to you. Not so soon after healing the betrayal from years ago."

"Thanks, I guess," Amacy said.

"Unfortunately, that leaves us at a bit of a loss. We don't have time for you to figure it out on your own. Brasmanathnon could break through the crust of the earth and terrorize Pennsylvania and beyond any day now. I'm too old to still worry about hurting you, but I do. And I've broken our only chance to get you where you need to be."

Amacy sighed. "I wish it were easier." She looked out across the snow and changed her mind. "No, more than that, I wish there were nothing to fix. That we could just be friends because we wanted to be and Tristan and I could just be in love, not destined to be together because we chose one another in a life long ago."

"Would you rather love someone else?"

Amacy frowned. “I don’t know. I don’t think I do. But I’d love to have the choice. Like anyone else.”

“What makes you think that anyone else’s choices aren’t as guided? Just because you know what caused yours and not others, does it make it less special? I would *die* to have what you have, and I don’t use that word lightly. There is no death for me. But if it were possible, I would take it just to have someone to love and to hold me forever.”

“You and Shrew aren’t...?”

Fiona laughed. “No, we’re not like you and Tristan. And since we are some of the only immortals left, it is very unlikely we will ever meet the ones for us.”

Amacy’s heart began to weep. “I’m so sorry.” Her eyes took up where her heart had started, and tears ran down her face. Outside in a Pennsylvania winter, her tears became icy immediately.

Fiona gave her a handkerchief, and she wiped her face, sniffling. “I’m sorry,” she said again, this time apologizing for her response.

“Think nothing of it. Someday, maybe Shrew and I won’t be needed to remind you of who you are for reasons beyond our petty desires to see you again and talk with people who understand. And then, we can just be friends because we want to, and you and Tristan can just be in love. But unfortunately, today is not that day. Today, we need to get you to find your powers and be able to use them. Because you will need them.”

Amacy leaned back and kicked her legs. Oh, to be back in a time when she hated this woman and worked at a dead-end job.

“Put this on,” Fiona said, holding out a gaudy necklace to her. It looked old, painfully old. The kind of thing that belonged in a museum. And definitely not around her neck. Large blue gems surrounded by smaller white stones that could be diamonds were joined together in ornately wrought silver. The conglomeration winked in the sun, dazzling her eyes.

She couldn't help the question. "Why?"

"Just like Tristan's sword, this necklace has been important to you in all your lives. It's possible that by wearing it, you will remember."

Amacy took it with gloved hands and drew it over her head, pushing the metal down the front of her coat and shirt to sit against her skin.

It was freezing cold, which was to be expected.

It warmed as it took heat from her body, but nothing else happened.

"I don't think it's going to help," she said to Fiona.

"I don't know if I'd agree," Fiona said. "Your ears are pointier and your eyes are black."

Amacy lifted a hand to her ear and found that what Fiona had said was true.

"Well, okay then but I don't feel any different. What is it supposed to do? What am I supposed to do?"

Fiona shrugged. "What is it that you want your magic to do for you?"

Amacy thought maybe she would like some of the trees to intertwine and turn into a trellis. But then she thought no, maybe that might be unkind to the trees. Her mind was so full of possibilities but none that seemed practical. Eventually, she sighed and said, "I don't know. Should I know?"

"Based on past experience, I haven't got a feckin' clue how your magic works, so maybe?"

That really wasn't helpful.

She frowned. "All I really want is to go back inside and get warm and drink the rest of my hot cocoa before my nose freezes off."

"We'd probably best make sure those two haven't broken all the furniture with the sword either," Fiona added. "Just... leave the necklace on for now. Like Tristan's sword, it will control what you see from others. Perhaps it will let the two of you get to know one another without your other selves getting in the way."

Fiona hadn't said it in a suggestive way, but Amacy still found her cheeks hot anyway. "Seems helpful I guess," she said, and followed Fiona back to the house.

"What are they going off to do?"

Shrew shrugged, reaching across Tristan to grab the sword. "Couldn't say." He fiddled with the hilt for a few minutes before adding, “Though if you hear screams, know that everything is okay.”

“Screams?” Tristan was growing worried.

Shrew stood with the sword and whirled it over his head before fluidly sitting once more. “Yeah. You shouldn’t have to worry too much on your end. Fighting is in your blood, and it looks like you’ve kept yourself in pretty good shape. The sword will remind you what to do, though. She does tend toward the long-suffering, so you may have to deal with a little sword snark mid-battle.”

The hair on Tristan’s arms stood up and he felt a jolt of bile try to escape his throat. “So...there’s no way to deal with this without fighting the dragon, huh?”

Shrew shook his head, silent.

“Let me ask you this, though. If the dragon is such a threat, why didn’t you and Fiona take it out while it was still small?”

Shrew proffered the sword back to Tristan, and he took it, strength infusing his body, vigor running through his veins.

“I’m a pacifist,” Shrew said. “There’s a reason my strongest magic is one that keeps me hidden, not one that hurts others. I’ve been alive for longer than anyone deserves to be. I’ve seen into the soul of who I am, and I am not a fighter. If I went into that mine, I would die. Fiona is spunkier than your average four-foot-nine woman, but she is still small. You saw how she was with the sword. She would trip over it and slice off her own foot. And then she would perish as well. And then there would be no one to warn you before it became the crisis point where your pet dragon was killing the world’s population, starting panic and possibly government action, revolts, and in essence, chaos.”

Tristan sighed, and lifted the tip of the sword from the floor, and held it before him, watching his reflection waver as it tried to find the right face from over the years to reflect. “What makes you think that Amacy and I will not perish?”

“There is no way to know. Every time you come back to help, there is always the danger that you might die, that you might fail. It is a risk you always take anyway. For the good of everyone.”

“How did we get to be so selfless?”

Shrew snorted, a sound of genuine humor. “Selfless? You think that is selfless?”

“Isn’t that the definition of selfless? Throwing yourself into danger and possibly death for the benefit of others?”

Shrew laughed and shook his head, then said, “Tristan, tell me. How many faces do you see in that sword?”

“What does that have to do with anything?”

“Just indulge me, will you?”

Tristan squinted at the sword's surface, but he couldn't tell. "I don't know. There's too many."

Shrew smiled. "Exactly. The average person, they think to themselves, this one life, that's all I've got. When I'm gone, I'm gone. You and Amacy, when you die, it may be a few years, but you get back up on your feet and you try again. But what happens if the planet is decimated? There are no people anymore? Nowhere good to live?"

Tristan didn't like where this was going.

"In those cases, you either do not get reborn or your life is so short you never know you were reborn. Just like everyone else, you don't want to die and you're willing to put your life on the line to protect your chances at living again. A non-standard fear of death, coming across as altruism, but with ones such as you and her, regular rules do not apply."

"Oh," Tristan said. "I hadn't considered that."

"Of course not," said Shrew. "One would always rather see themselves as a hero than a craven bastard. I came to terms with my own craven bastard nature long ago, so it is much easier for me to point it out in others. But sometimes, the thing that people call bravery can come from a bed of fear. We craven bastards have been doing stupid shit to save our own necks for as long as there have been people to misinterpret our actions as bravery."

Shrew clapped his hands to his knees loudly and stood up. "Let's go drink some coffee and look at some mine maps. Doesn't that sound like an exciting time?"

* * *

Amacy and Fiona came back in to find Tristan and Shrew in the kitchen sipping hot drinks. Amacy snagged Tristan's mug but quickly returned it when she realized that he'd added so much milk to his coffee that it was just lukewarm. "Blech," she said and went in search of the rest of her mug of hot chocolate to try to reheat it in the microwave. She didn't much like reheated cocoa, but she needed something.

"What are you two doing?" she asked, mug in hand, leaning over Shrew's shoulder.

"These are the maps of the mine below Centralia from when it was still in operation," Shrew said. "We have no way of knowing what it looks like now. Brasmanathnon has no doubt done some rearranging where he's chewed through the rock for the coal. But it is nice to get a starting point."

"Makes sense," she said, sitting down at the table next to him.

Fiona joined Tristan on the other side.

Amacy said, “What I don’t understand is exactly what you expect of us. Do you mean us to kill him? I don’t know if I can. None of this is really his fault. He didn’t ask to be hatched. He didn’t ask for us to raise him and then abandon him. Doesn’t he deserve a chance at life?”

Fiona smirked. “You truly never change,” she said. “Those words could have come from Alma’s mouth.”

“That is certainly the *easiest* way of dealing with him,” Shrew said.

“Saying it that way implies there are other options. Harder options. What are those?”

“Well, for one, you could try to go in and try to explain to him why you abandoned him and how what he’s doing is going to hurt people and hope he cares. That would be much harder,” said Fiona. “In fact, I would posit that one is so hard you might want to categorize it as impossible. We still don’t know if he has intellect. From what you told us about him, after you admitted what you had done, he seemed more animalistic than other dragons we'd met. So, chances are if you tried that, he would merely attack and you would return to the having-to-kill-him-part."

Amacy said, "Okay, so there's a fallback if it seems he's intelligent. Anything else?"

Shrew and Fiona looked at one another for a moment, holding a silent conversation with their eyes.

Willing to wait for them to conclude their silent conversation, Amacy took a sip from her mug. She realized too late as the cool ceramic touched her lips that she had forgotten to microwave it. But when the liquid hit her mouth, it was not cold but hot. That perfect temperature for hot beverages between "I just burned the length of my esophagus" and "this isn't very hot."

Surprised, she accidentally inhaled a little and ended up coughing violently with

Shrew smacking her back and asking, "You okay?"

When she got her breathing under control, she laughed and said, "My hot chocolate was hot."

Tristan raised an eyebrow. "Isn't that what hot chocolate is meant to be?"

"Yes, but it's been sitting in the kitchen for about an hour. It shouldn't be."

She caught Fiona's smile. Relief filled her. "Does that mean...?" She didn't finish her question.

Fiona nodded. "It's the small, unconscious stuff that comes first. Things you desire will often just happen for you."

"Well, right now I desire to know what the other hard option that you aren't telling us is, but I have a feeling that won't just happen for me."

Fiona shrugged, then waved a hand toward Shrew and said, "You may as well tell them."

He nodded. "There's a reason we are looking at this map even though it's most likely no longer accurate. You're aware that dragon souls cannot be reborn in our world, correct?"

Amacy wasn't certain she had been aware of that before. "I am now."

"Ah, all right. Well. With the lack of the correct vessel, a dragon body, the realm which houses other souls between lives has nowhere to put them. So, another realm formed. Just for dragons. They live and die and are reborn there. And at one time, it was possible to open portals between our world and theirs. In the past, there have also been natural ones. Usually in caves.

"*If* it is still possible, we were hoping to find a likely cave for you to lure him to and open the portal. There are some potential problems with this, which is why we weren't sure if we should tell you and get your hopes up. One—if you open the portal and it is in an inhabited area on the other side, it is possible that more dragons could come through and then we would be in quite a pickle. And two—it may not even work. Magic in our world is dissipating. You may not have the power to do it.

"Three—we don't know how to do it, so we can't tell you. *You* have done it before, when you sent away Chuck after it was obvious that he would no longer be reborn. But in order to do it, you would have to have some feat of memory, and we aren't sure how to trigger that kind of epiphany. Since Fiona already failed to bring the lion's share back by making you believe your life is in danger, we can't really do much more to help you there."

"If magic is dissipating...what does that mean for you?"

"Exactly what you think it does," said Fiona. "We will die. But you have to admit—we've already lived lives that others would kill to have."

Amacy frowned. Though that was true, she still didn't want to think of her friends dying. It somehow didn't seem right. To have lived this long only to fade into nothing.

"Did we leave journals? Instructions? Grimoires? Anything?"

Fiona shook her head. "Nothing written has survived. Upon your deaths, you had us burn all easily taken evidence so that outsiders wouldn't get their hands on it. You only ever left with us the things you knew no one else could access the knowledge in, the sword and the necklace."

Amacy shook her head, then smacked the table and stood up. "God damn it, I'll think of something. No one should have to die. We live to protect others, and that should mean Brasmanathnon too. He's our responsibility, but it's not our responsibility to kill him. It can't be. Our responsibility to him hasn't changed since we forced life upon him. We are meant to care for him, to teach him, not murder him because we can't figure out how to take care of him anymore. We need to learn to match his needs, he is not required to fit his needs to what we understand."

She turned and stalked out of the kitchen, heading upstairs to the bedroom. She needed to think.

Tristan's eyes widened. He was surprised to see Amacy had such strong feelings on the subject of the dragon. To him, the idea of going into the mine and killing it was so nebulous he could not form opinions about it. What had they done to Amacy? And why hadn't they done it to him too? He *wanted* to know what was going on. To care. To have a strong stance.

He got up from the table and followed Amacy out of the kitchen and up the stairs to their room. Amacy was just closing the door when Tristan put a hand on it to stop it.

“Let me in,” he said.

Amacy stopped the pressure on the door and moved away but didn’t open the door any farther. Tristan wasn’t sure if that meant to come in or not. He pushed the door open, walked in, and then closed it behind him.

“Are you okay?”

Amacy sat on the bed, looking tired. “Just overwhelmed.”

Tristan sat down next to her and hesitantly put an arm around her. Amacy leaned into him, and he put his head on top of hers, a calm pleasure filling him at their closeness without the shadows of their other selves intruding.

“I just can’t stomach the idea that our only option is to kill him,” Amacy said.

“I’m not all for killing him either. What you said in the kitchen was true. It wasn’t his fault that he's alive. But aren't the lives of others worth more than his? We know he has killed before. He will kill again. We should stop it before we have any more blood on our hands."

Amacy stiffened against Tristan, and he couldn't sure if she truly didn't agree or if she just didn't want to agree. He didn't release her, though. He wouldn't allow a mistake from over a hundred years ago to drive them apart.

"Something has been wrong about this since the start," he said. "Every memory I have about him feels oily, wrong. I think something more was going on than either of us know. And it's possible that the others know and just aren't telling us. I think someone was influencing me back then. I think someone made me steal the egg and forced me to not listen to you when you said we shouldn't hatch it."

Amacy pulled back and looked at him. "Really? Why didn't you mention this before?"

"What if the source of the influence was one of our 'friends' downstairs?"

Amacy's face went white. "They know so much about us, but we know next to nothing about them. What if you're right?"

Tristan shook her head. "I don't know. I've been trying to figure that out too. I just can't figure out why either of them would want to wake a dragon, though. We've no doubt by now both seen flashes of the four of us. We've all been together forever. I'm not sure I can believe that one of them would have done so, but at the same time, it's as you said. We know nothing about them. Not really."

"Well, if it was one of them, it couldn't be Fiona. She gave me this necklace," she said, pulling the object from the front of her shirt.

It was large and gaudy, and Tristan wasn't sure why jewelry might mean innocence.

"Since I've put it on, I've been able to see things more clearly and understand things about our past lives more quickly. It makes me feel right for the first time since this all started."

She was silent for a moment before she said, "But I don't remember seeing it in any of the memories I've had so far. It's meant to help bring back my magic. If I didn't have it, I couldn't have stopped whatever was happening to you."

Tristan frowned. This admission did not bode well.

"Fiona said they messed up last time somehow. Maybe they noticed something was off with you too but couldn't figure out where it was coming from so assumed they'd just woken us too early?"

"I don't know," Tristan said. "I don't know what to think. So many things they've said and done seem to disprove that they set us up, but they've had plenty of time to come up with a story that we'd believe. What if they've been controlling us through what information they choose to share?”

She leaned against Tristan again and pulled him into her side. “I don’t know,” she said.

* * *

That night, after a dinner that was slightly more tense than it probably needed to be, Amacy and Tristan went back to their room.

“I don’t want to sleep by myself tonight,” Amacy said.

She could see the fear on his face right away and it made her sad. He should never have to fear her.

“I don’t mean sex,” she said. She wouldn’t object to such a useful stress-reliever, but she could see he was not ready yet, and she was willing to give him time. But that didn’t mean they couldn’t be intimate in other ways.

They had gone to bed with their clothes on the night before, but she had packed pajamas and meant to use them tonight. She unbuttoned her shirt and pulled it off, then pulled on her pajama top and repeated the procedure with her pants.

When she turned back to him, he was blushing.

She touched his cheek and turned her back. "I'll let you change without watching, if you prefer."

She unhooked her bra and pulled it out her sleeve, dropping it on the floor.

"I don't own pajamas," he said.

Amacy crawled into the bed and pulled up the covers. "Well, come on, then. Boxers or whatever you're wearing. Doesn't matter to me. Just come keep me warm."

After a moment, he pulled off his shirt and pants and joined her, his boxer-briefs defining his quite attractive butt for a moment before they disappeared beneath the covers.

"I left the necklace on so we shouldn't be bothered by memories if our skin were to touch in the night."

He lay like a board, not touching her, not speaking. She squirmed across the bed and lay so their arms touched. He reached out his fingers, and they entwined with hers. Sweet if awkward. Hesitantly, she rolled onto her side and slid her hand across his chest as she put her arm around him, capturing their hands between them. His other arm came up and rested across her shoulder.

He was willing to take the initiative in small things like that. That made her glad. He did want her even if he was afraid.

She tilted her head back and kissed him gently where his jawbone met his neck. His skin was soft beneath her lips, and she wanted to linger there, but she let her head drop back down and snuggled her ear against his chest. His heart beat quickly, and after a moment, he shifted, rolling onto his side and moving her gently so that they lay front-to-front, their noses touching. She stared into his gray eyes and he into her brown and without truly knowing who initiated it, suddenly their lips touched, and she never wanted to do anything else but lay with him forever, bodies entwined, lips on one another. He shifted again, and his upper body was over hers, his arm cradling her head against the pillow.

Her breath came faster as their kiss deepened. The angle was awkward, though, and she pulled at his waist until he moved his hips on top of hers, their bodies pressed up against one another. Despite the fear on his face at the thought of sex, his body was certainly ready.

She pulled back a little and murmured, "I know what I said earlier, but if you decide to disregard, I'm fine with that too."

He gave a light laugh, and that ignited such a desire in her that she pulled up her head to meet his and their lips met once again. She took his hand not supporting his weight and ran it up under her shirt. He touched her nipple with his cold fingertips, and she couldn't stop the gasp against his lips. He gave a light groan in response, and his hand explored both her breasts then ran down over her side onto her back. He leaned his weight onto that arm then released his other from behind her head, breaking their mouths from one another's to do so. He pulled their bodies apart slightly and reached his arm down over her stomach and down the waistband of her pajama pants. He fumbled for the band of her panties as well, but then his hand slid under and found the mound between her legs. Gently parting her lower lips, he rubbed his finger over her clitoris then up inside her. She arched her back and gasped. He kissed down the side of her neck as he stroked his finger inside her.

He pulled up the edge of her pajama shirt with his teeth as she began to pant. His mouth found her breast and her nipple, and she couldn't hold back a moan. As he suckled and stroked, she found the front of his underpants and pulled out his silky soft erection, stroking it in the same rhythm he stroked her.

He moaned deeply and came up for air. "We need these clothes off," he said.

She couldn't agree more. He pulled his hand from her pants, and she scrambled to remove her pajamas in record time. When they came back together, she wore nothing but the necklace, his soft skin against hers, the tip of his erection pressing against her as though asking for entry. She fought the urge to slide herself onto him. For all she knew, this was his first time and he should be in control for that. They lay there for a moment, panting and aching, before Tristan thrust forward and entered her. They both moaned. Their bodies fit together perfectly. He pressed into her deep G-spot with every stroke and soon she was clawing at the sheets, not even trying to quiet the sounds ripping from her throat.

They moved together until orgasm ripped through her, followed quickly by a deep thrust by him and a moan.

They panted together, kissing each other's sweaty faces as the cool air around them reasserted itself.

They rolled apart to air their sweaty skin but kept their hands clasped together.

She looked over at him, and the light of the moon through the window glinted across his eyes, and she knew they would get very little sleep that night. He reached across the bed and pulled her back to him, their mouths meeting once more.

Chapter 12

Centralia, Pennsylvania, January 03

The morning came too soon. Tristan woke, naked and cold, limbs entwined with Amacy's, sheets somewhere else. He disentangled himself from Amacy, and she slept on. He found one of the blankets and laid it over her before using a second as a toga to get himself to the bathroom.

The feeling of power and rightness from the night before was gone, and in the morning light filtering through the tiny bathroom window, he was just a man once more, no longer part of something bigger.

Had his decision to have sex with Amacy been the right one? He didn't regret it at all, but part of him wondered if he should have waited until their real selves had come to the conclusion that they should do so.

But had he not?

When they touched last night, no one else had been inside his mind but him.

He stepped into the shower and washed all his confusion and uncertainty down the drain. He washed off the old Tristan's fear of being seen as an invalid. His old fear of being crazy. He washed off his fear of intimate situations and the certainty that he would not be satisfactory in bed. Down the drain went all the things that had been part of himself that he no longer needed. In their place was a bright bubble of possibility.

This morning, he would listen to the sword, and he would let it teach him all the things part of him already knew but had forgotten.

Downstairs was empty. Bright light streamed in the bank of windows over the kitchen sink. It felt as though he were completely alone. Just him in the farmhouse in the middle of nowhere. Perhaps he was the only person in the world. It was a strangely freeing feeling.

He took a cup of coffee from the still-warm carafe and wondered where their handlers had gone. He went to the front hall and looked out to the parking area out front. Amacy's car sat next to the blue Mini and Fiona's green Beetle. It was a strange grouping of cars. All so old in a modern world. Just like their owners.

He turned to go back to the kitchen and jumped because Fiona stood directly behind him, blinking at him through a pair of magnifying lenses. She pulled them up her face onto her head and said, "Oh. We didn't expect either of you up so early."

He blushed, realizing that they could probably hear every sound that had come from their room the night before.

Fiona patted his elbow in a motherly way, and with it came little sparks of memory. Fiona wrapping a wound. Fiona handing him a bowl of steaming soup while he lay in bed.

It seemed so unlikely that a woman like that would betray them by forcing the situation. But if it hadn't been her, it could have been Shrew.

"Where's Shrew?" He tried to sound casual but suspected he didn't.

"Same place I just was. Come on. I came up for coffee, but you may as well join us. Will was pretty good at what we're working at, so maybe you can offer some insights."

He followed her into the kitchen, where she poured two mugs of coffee, then led him back to the front hall. She went behind the welcome desk and opened a section of the paneled wall with a knob hidden within a mailbox cubby.

She started down the stairs behind the wall.

He reached back and shut the door before following her down the stairs. The floor at the bottom was unfinished dirt. His feet chilled on contact, and he wished that she had warned him to put on shoes. Several tables were set up with chemistry paraphernalia. The walls were built with shelves piled with bottles and flasks and pouches of things.

“Science and magic go hand-in-hand,” Fiona explained. “At one time, you were very good at figuring out chemical compounds that would help to enhance magic.”

Shrew silently pipetted something into a flask under a naked bulb hanging from the ceiling.

“We’re trying to come up with a way to enhance Amacy’s magic to give her the chance, if she can take it, to open the portal," Fiona explained. "We want to give you as many options as possible going in. I hope she can remember."

Shrew put the flask over a Bunsen burner then came over to them, taking his mug from Fiona.

"It is not as helpful as it used to be. The science doesn't help as much. And the magic doesn't help the science as much. But it is still there."

They sipped their coffee in silence, the icy cold from beneath Tristan's feet seeping up into his legs.

"If you open yourself up to possibility, I believe you should be able to identify components that will help us," Fiona said.

"What does that mean?"

"Wander around the room. Look at everything. If something feels right, bring it to the table and we'll try it."

He did so, wondering as he wandered, if he should trust their judgement.

He brought several things to the table when he felt the urge to pick them up. When he was done, he had piled a bunch of unfamiliar items on the table.

Fiona inspected them and looked up at him. “These are the ingredients for magic-enhancing war paint.”

“Effective?”

Fiona nodded. “But there’s an extra ingredient. I guess we’ll try it to see what it does.”

“Just don’t blow up the house,” Tristan said and retreated from the basement, the cold and the strangeness too much for him.

* * *

Amacy was standing in the kitchen, staring out the windows. He wanted to come up behind her and slide his hands around her waist and kiss her neck, but despite what they had done the night before, he still felt strangely shy and around her.

He settled for saying, “Good morning,” in his sultriest voice.

Which was not actually sultry at all.

I’m terrible at this.

She turned and smiled. “I’d wondered where everyone had gone.”

She came to him and leaned her head against his shoulder, which he took to mean he should put his arms around her. He did.

“Fiona and Shrew are cooking up some sort of magic enhancer in the basement in hopes it will help you cast the spell to open the portal.”

She murmured against his chest, seemingly unwilling to be quite awake yet.

"What?" He didn't really care what she'd said; he wanted her to stay in his arms, but he didn't want to seem as though he ignored what she said.

She pulled back, which made him sad. "That's what they *say* they're doing, you mean."

Back to reality. "True. Though they did have me do a free search of their supplies. Apparently, my last self was a magical chemist. Though now that I think of it, that could have been an attempt to deflect me from paying attention to what they were doing."

Amacy made a dismissive sound, as though she didn't agree.

"Which part is the 'hmph' for?"

"I don't know." She pulled away from him completely. "I can't decide if they're manipulating us or not. Fiona seems genuine. And the way Shrew looks at his plant and gets all embarrassed when I make fun of his sprightly nature, he doesn't seem to have a malicious bone in his body. What if it wasn't them and some other outside source influencing you in the past? What if we could have had the chance to ask them about it and never take it and end up dying because of it?"

Dying. He'd tried so hard not to think about that possibility. But they were Japan and they were going up against Godzilla.

He sighed. "I guess you're right. Nothing good ever came from holding back information. I should talk to them."

He started toward the hallway and the basement door.

Then the earth began to shake.

Not the gentle rattling he'd experienced twice before, but a rolling thrusting as though the earth were a dog after a bath, trying to shake the houses free of its skin.

"Get in the doorway," he shouted over the rattle of the house. "In these older houses, it's the strongest part of the structure."

Amacy stumbled to the doorway, and he followed after her.

The geologic violence went on for only moments, but as they clung to one another and the wood of the doorway, it felt like ages.

Finally, the world stopped moving.

The silence surrounding them was deafening.

"It's like he was right below us," Amacy whispered, as though afraid the dragon would hear them.

Tristan hurried to the door of the basement and pulled it open. "You okay down there?"

No answer came.

He glanced to Amacy and then turned to the basement, irrational fear already setting in.

“Shrew? Fiona?”

No one replied. It was warm. Warmer than he remembered.

At the bottom of the stairs was a crack three feet across.

No one remained in the basement.

“Shit. Shit shit shit. Shit.”

He stood frozen, staring at the gaping hole. Should he get closer? Was Brasmananthnon right below, mouth open, ready for him to fall in?

He turned and ran back up the stairs.

“They’re gone. There’s a hole in the floor. Holy fuck, they’re gone.”

Amacy rushed to the living room where Tristan’s sword had been leaning against the side of the couch, now lying on the floor after the earthquake. Tristan trailed along behind her, obviously still befuddled by whatever he saw in the basement.

She thrust the sword at him. “We have to go look for them. Make sure they aren’t hurt and vulnerable where the dragon could reach them.”

He took it, and she hurried back toward the basement, but at the last minute, she thought of Shrew’s plant. If the plant made him tall and robust when it was healthy, surely if he were badly hurt or… otherwise, then the plant would reflect that?

She ran to the living room. The pot lay smashed on the floor, the dirt maintaining its shape only by the roots holding it together. It looked sad somehow, and the healthy glow around it was gone. But it wasn’t dead, thank goodness. *What if the fall would have broken the stalk? Would that have meant death?*

She picked up the plant and looked for something else to put it in, cradling it like a baby.

“Help me find a new pot,” she shouted to Tristan, still distraught and wandering behind her like a small dog not sure if it was supposed to bark at an intruder or not. He turned and headed out of the room. At least the importance of this made it into his mind.

She rummaged through the kitchen cabinets one-handed and was about to put it in a cooking pot when Tristan came in with a large pot, so heavy it nearly dragged between his legs. “This was in the hall closet,” he said.

She had him set it on the floor near the bank of windows, hoping that the frail winter sun would be enough for it until they returned. She set the root ball gently into the pot and wondered if Shrew had been intending to replant the potato here. It looked awkward and only half-done. She considered asking Tristan if there was a bag of soil in the closet as well, but they didn't have time. And heaven knew she didn't know how to pot a plant. She'd probably kill the thing, and that would have much more dire consequences than killing a regular houseplant.

On impulse, she kissed the little leaf at the top of the curling stem, and it seemed as though the leaves below reached up toward her. She pulled away.

"Keep healthy," she told the plant.

Maybe it was the light of the sun in the windows, but she thought maybe a little of its former glow had returned.

Finally, they hurried back to the basement door. Suddenly cautious, she hung back. Could the dragon have slithered up and out of the crack while they had been above? How big was he?

Tristan took her hand, and they looked at one another for a long moment. Neither of them was ready, but the situation had brought them to a point where they couldn't turn back. He leaned in and kissed her softly on the lips, then released her hand and started down the steps.

It was quiet below. It hadn't been loud upstairs, but there was a hush in the basement that didn't seem altogether natural. She felt disinclined to speak because she had the feeling that someone was listening.

Waiting.

Tristan tested each stair before putting his weight on them and as she got past the angled part of the ceiling that was also the bottom of the steps to the floor above, she could see why. The gash through the floor dug out the space below the last few steps. Unless the stair assemblage was sturdy, the whole of the stairwell could fall into it at any moment.

Partway down, Tristan leaped over the edge onto the unbroken portion of floor and momentarily looked surprised. She looked down and realized that neither of them was wearing shoes. She signaled for Tristan to wait and hurried back up the stairs, finding both their shoes in the hallway where they'd left them, then ran back to Tristan. She was still in her pajamas, but it just wasn't to be helped. At least she'd showered before she'd come down. Her mother would be so disappointed if she went into a dangerous situation without clean underwear.

She crouched down and tossed Tristan's to him and then put on her own. Pajamas, no socks, and sneakers. Absolutely the outfit of an avenging warrior.

As was Tristan's button-down and nice slacks. With no socks.

Warriors didn't need socks. Socks were just a hinderance.

She was pretty certain the proximity to the opening to the mines was making her a little panicky, making her brain run off where it wanted as long as she didn't make it think about their situation.

She tied her sneakers and then jumped over the railing to join Tristan on the floor. Nothing like a little parkour to start the day.

He took her hand, and they approached the edge of the broken dark earth of the basement floor.

They peered over the edge, but the crevice was too dark to see inside. It was impossible to tell how deep the crack was, but since Shrew's plant wasn't dead, it couldn't be too deep, right?

She wasn't sure she could talk herself into jumping down inside with them, though.

Tristan turned and went to the table behind them, grabbing a little stoppered bottle and a little pouch. Those must have been the items he'd said the others had been working on earlier. At least they'd finished before the earth had swallowed them.

She was about to join Tristan, to whisper to him that they should search for a flashlight or something when her foot started to slide. It wasn't that the edge had become slippery or she had become clumsy, but the dirt below her had begun to give way. She wanted to shout, but something told her that that would be a disastrous idea. She turned and tried to throw herself to the ground, but the damage had already been done. Her foot was already in the empty air below. She slid into the hole trying to grab something, but failing.

And then she was falling.

Tristan wasn't sure if the bottle and the pouch were finished items or just ingredients, but he figured they couldn't hurt to have. He grabbed them from the table and slipped them in the pockets of his slacks. When he turned around, Amacy was gone.

He hurried to the edge of the rent and stopped when he noticed the dirt sliding down into the hole near where she had been. He stepped back, revealing a handprint where she had attempted to keep herself from falling. Why hadn't she shouted?

Had she been grabbed? On the edge of panic, he paced at the edge of the crevice. Should he jump in too and hope that he lived at the bottom? Amacy had been convinced that Shrew's plant meant that he was still alive. If he had survived... maybe Amacy was below, waiting for him. And by hanging out up here prevaricating, he was leaving her alone in the dark. *In the dark.*

He looked around for a flashlight. Candles. Anything that would give light. Shrew had lit the Bunsen burner with something earlier. Matches even.

He found an electric lantern at the bottom of one of the rickety shelves. After an experimental flick of the on/off button, he decided the light output was good enough. He moved to the edge and stood there, exceptionally aware he held a bare sword in one hand and a lantern in the other, and had a glass bottle in his pocket. And he was about to willingly fall down a hole.

His life had come to this.

From someone whom everyone deemed to be crazy because of how he saw the world to someone whom he would call crazy for thinking that jumping down a hole in a near-stranger's basement was anything other than ludicrous.

He chose a spot farther along the jagged rift than Amacy's ominous handprint and sat down on the ground, holding the sword in an uncertain grip.

It's now or never.

He pushed himself forward, feet-first, over the edge.

Chapter 13

Below, January 03

It was dark. Completely dark. Amacy couldn't even see the light from above. It was like falling into a completely different world. She stood up stiffly and brushed herself off. It hadn't exactly been like falling on a pile of pillows, but it also wasn't as bad as she'd expected.

She scuffed a shoe along the floor. It was strangely soft. And there was very little sound. So here she was in a room undoubtedly filled with entrails or something just as hideous with no sound and no light and no one else. In pink fleece pajamas and sneakers and a necklace worth probably more than her entire apartment building's rent for thirty-five years.

If she hadn't been certain silence was important, she would have started to laugh and perhaps never stopped. It was so ridiculous and horrible that she wanted to sit down and cry. But Shrew and Fiona had fallen down here as well, and they had kept going, so she would too.

And then a light clicked on.

It made a gentle *pop* and then was there, behind her. It was blinding after the total dark.

"Amacy." Tristan's voice came in a hiss, and in a second, the atmosphere of the place was different. It was immediately less oppressive. As though the environment itself was glad he'd come. And that quickly, she was no longer certain she should stay silent.

“Tristan,” she replied, hurrying across the soft floor, her eyes searching him for injuries. His hair was disheveled, his glasses askew, but otherwise he appeared unharmed.

Her knight in slacks and button-down.

She threw her arms around him, and, above her head, he raised the lantern. He used the other arm to wrap around her, the cold length of the sword against her back. “We appear to be in a cave completely mossed over. I suppose if we were going to fall anywhere, this would be the place.”

Amacy pulled back from him and glanced around the cave. He was right.

“There must be some sort of entrance somewhere to give the moss enough light to flourish, but it’s hard to say which way that might be.”

A horrible thought hit Amacy. “Do you think Shrew and Fiona found the way out and have already escaped?”

But then again, when she had been alone, there had been no light at all. Definitely not enough to make all the moss grow. She frowned. Something was really not right here, but she wasn't sure how to explain her unease.

She still couldn't help but feel that they had passed out of their own world and into another.

"Which way should we go?" She looked up and down the corridor, only wide enough for them to hold hands, and stretch out their arms, and touch the walls. Either way seemed just as promising as the other, but for some reason, the dark way before them beckoned to her rather than the darkness behind.

"Ahead?" Tristan's question confirmed her desire.

"Let's go then."

"Wait," he said. He patted his pockets, then set down the lantern and pulled two small items out. "Fiona and Shrew were making these when the floor broke. I think they're finished."

Amacy held out a hand. "What are these?"

Tristan placed a small pouch and a small vial in her palm. "I think they're supposed to enhance magic. One is supposedly war-paint with some sort of enhancement. I don't know what enhancement, and I don't know which one is the paint."

Shaking her head, Amacy uncorked the bottle and dipped a finger in it. The substance inside was blue. She drew a circle on one cheek with it. She re-corked the bottle and stowed it in her pajama pockets, then tried the pouch. This one was yellow. She drew a triangle on the other cheek.

"Well, whatever it's for, I'm all painted up. Let's get this over with."

The path they followed varied little, and Amacy began to have doubts, remembering the worm from the movie *Labyrinth* admonishing the main character she could have reached her goal if only she would have turned the other way.

There didn't seem to be any visible tracks like one would have with flattened grass or footprints in dust. Could one leave tracks in moss? She didn't know.

She eyed the lantern from time to time, watching for signs that it would wear out, hoping the battery was well-charged.

As it was, traveling in a bubble of moveable light was almost unbearably creepy. She couldn't imagine how horrible it would be without light altogether.

She touched the wall experimentally, just in case she ended up having to use its presence to lead her on. She hoped it wasn't gross. The wall felt like sticking one's hand in raw hamburger to mix up meatballs.

Shrew stumbled along, hand to the wall, leading Fiona through the suffocating darkness.

Behind her, a *click*, and she came back to the present. At least they were on the right trail. But she couldn't figure out why Tristan had turned off the lantern.

She was startled to realize that little sparkling stars of light amongst the moss illuminated the path a few feet in front of them and behind in a soft glow.

Fabulous. Not only was it nasty, but she had to touch it to reveal the path Shrew left behind.

Just to confirm, she took her hand away from the wall, and the light around them faded like the afterglow of a fluorescent light powering down.

Wish I would have known to bring rubber gloves. My hands are going to prune so bad.

They kept along, Amacy dragging her fingers through the moist fronds of moss.

“They passed this way,” she said, her voice low and quiet, muffled by the soft moss around them.

“You can tell?”

She nodded. “Yeah. I’m not sure what caused it since the necklace is supposed to suppress unbidden memories. But I saw them going the same way. It’s like they left their memories there for me to find or something.”

Tristan made a noncommittal noise, and she was pretty sure he was wondering the same thing she was. Had they somehow planted the memories that they had seen of each other? That seemed less likely, especially since she had had some in dreams, and surely, they couldn’t have triggered those?

They kept walking, making very little sound as they shuffled along.

“The moss,” Tristan said eventually. “It wouldn’t be here if the dragon had been along this corridor.”

Amacy stopped and frowned. Had he been right below them at all? It was so hard to know what was real anymore.

She took her hands from the wall and plunged the pair of them into darkness, ignoring the gentle protests from Tristan. She breathed deeply, and the moist, earthy scent filled her nostrils. There was nothing of stone here, just moss and life. And with the scent was linked a memory. Sprites and nature were intertwined to such an extent that plants could call up nature even where it did not belong. She had a sudden feeling that behind them, the moss would be dead, returned to the earth it was created from.

“They’re leaving us a trail,” she said.

She touched the wall, and the lights came back, the glow so like that which had surrounded Shrew's potato plant she was surprised she hadn't connected the two before.

She glanced around, getting a feel for the size of the tunnel. "At least he can't be very big," she said, not giving voice to the reality that twice their size was still quite large.

Tristan made a light *tsk* sound. She wasn't sure what that sound was supposed to mean, but she kept on.

Ahead, the light cut out and a soft whisper of a breeze touched her face. Such movement of air felt eerie, impossible, this far below the surface. The tunnel converged, leaving two equally dark options.

"Switch on the lantern," she said, the little hairs on the back of her neck standing on end. She already felt deeply that something was wrong.

Tristan obligingly did, and ahead, in the path, lay a charred skeleton, reaching its arm out toward them as though they could pull it to safety.

Amacy put a hand over her mouth to stifle her sharp intake of breath.

Oh, man, I am so not ready for this. Jesus.

Tristan didn't think he'd hit his head when he fell, but ever since he'd arrived, he hadn't been able to shake a weird buzz from between his ears. And the skeleton before him merely heightened the whine.

He nestled the sword in the crook of his elbow and reached out for Amacy.

"What if it's one of them?" She whispered it, but the question arrested him. "The moss stops here. Is that Shrew?"

Desperate to comfort her, to tell her it wasn't true, he lifted the lantern. But there was no moss to be seen. Since the moss had come from Shrew, it was completely possible that this skeleton was his.

“I don’t know,” he said with a shrug.

“So, which way do we go?” Her tone turned from horrified to businesslike in a matter of moments. As though she had decided to ignore the body. An understandable choice. No sense worrying about that when they were planning on heading into the beast’s lair to do battle with it. They couldn’t afford to become emotionally compromised over someone they barely knew and may have lured them here.

He ignored the body as well, already a feeling of ease coming over him with the decision. He bounced from foot to foot, not sure how to answer her question. But then the buzzing lessened and he could feel again. Just as something had drawn him down here, this direction made him want to turn to the left. The right sloped upward, the left downward. It made sense that they would want to continue down.

"Left?"

Her question seemed to coincide with his thoughts.

"Seems like a good choice," he said.

She nodded and stepped out into the cross way, seeming to not even see the corpse. But then, as though on impulse, she reached down and pressed a hand to a blackened arm bone.

She gasped, then gave him a strange look and stood up. "Let's go."

What was the look for? Had it meant that it was Shrew? He didn't know and if it did, didn't want to ask and upset her.

He followed her down the passageway, the light of the lantern illuminating wooden beams here and there. "We're in the original mine now, aren't we?"

"I think so, yes," she responded, her voice flat. She seemed subdued. The skeleton must have been Shrew. He reached out to touch her, but she brushed him away.

He did not try again.

As they descended, the air became warmer. He adjusted his grip on the lantern so he could push his sleeves up as far as the buttons would allow. “The mine is still on fire, isn’t it?” The thought was not comforting. How could they deal with a dragon let alone a dragon surrounded by fire?

Amacy did not look at him. “And apparently Brasmanathnon has only made it worse. How do you feel?”

The question blindsided him. He touched his head, unconsciously. There must be a bump on his head or something. He opened his mouth to say, “I think I hit my head,” but what came out was, “I’m fine.”

He frowned. That wasn’t true at all. What had made him say the other thing?

He was too tired to think about it. They walked on in silence.

* * *

Something was wrong with Tristan. Though neither of them really knew Shrew a great deal in this life, it was still quite a shock to find a skeleton that might be him. And Tristan had brushed it off as though nothing had happened. She'd tested him with her feigned disinterest. And he had just gone along with it. And he had never even asked if the vision she'd had was of Shrew.

It hadn't been. Which was the only reason she was still holding it together. The vision hadn't made any sense, though. The man had run from an exploding Zeppelin. There was no reason he should have expired here, underground. But he wasn't Shrew. Though the vision had changed at the end to one of Shrew, illuminated in a similar glow to that of the moss in the tunnel, touching the same set of bones, a motion as though inserting something into them. And his voice. "Don't trust your thoughts; trust your instincts."

He had been alone, making her concerned for Fiona. She also wished he had given her instruction on where they'd gone.

And on top of all that, she couldn't trust Tristan.

They kept along the tunnel. and her shoulders itched. She was all too aware that Tristan was right behind her with a sword. He could end her life with as little thought as he gave to the corpse that might have been Shrew's.

"Why don't you come up here and walk next to me? There's plenty of room," she said when she couldn't stand him behind her anymore.

She slowed a little to let him catch up, but he did not come to her side. "I want to stay behind you so I can illuminate our way easier. If I'm next to you, there might be something in your path the light wouldn't pick up."

Though his answer sounded reasonable, it left her chilled, even in the heightening heat. *He's herding me. He's making sure I can't go back. Am I to be a sacrifice then?*

There wasn't much to do but go on. She didn't want to fight him, and if she did, it could be her own thoughts that were faulty, not his.

Something glimmered with an icy white light ahead, and she hurried to it before the lantern could completely illuminate it. A pure white daffodil with a white stem grew from the floor along the wall, giving off the light. It was so beautiful it made her heart ache. She would have to compliment Shrew on his handiwork when they made it out.

Had he left a memory inside it? She caressed the edge of the ruffly flower with her fingertip, and it was enough to send her somewhere else for a few seconds.

Dragons, flying above. Something rustles in the grass nearby. A small child with wolf ears stares down at the flower, picks it, and blows the seeds away like a dandelion.

Shrew hadn't left this flower. The vision associated with it meant nothing to her. What she had seen could have been from a completely different world.

Tristan stood beside her, silent, and she considered discussing what she'd seen, but she decided against it. He didn't seem in the mood for curiosity.

"It's beautiful, isn't it? I wouldn't have expected something so lovely to grow down here." She stood, dusting off the seat of her pajama pants, reminding herself of her attire.

"I've read somewhere that most cave-dwelling things are pure white and sometimes produce their own light. It is quite striking though." He angled out the sword tip and sliced the flower from its leaves, the light going out. He picked it up and presented it to her. "A lovely flower for a lovely lady."

She wanted to recoil at the needless killing, but she forced herself to take it. Perhaps there were seeds inside she could bring to the surface where its descendants could live in the sun once more.

She tucked it into the band of her messy ponytail. A talisman. She would get back out alive.

Amacy's stomach growled, reminding her that she hadn't eaten anything that morning. Her legs ached, and it felt as though they had walked for an entire week. She wanted to sit down, but nowhere seemed particularly inviting.

"He must have shaken the earth then run to have gotten so far ahead of us," Amacy said, unable to keep the complaint to herself.

"This path will lead us to him," Tristan replied, his inflection flat and matter of fact. The lantern-light showed the dreamy look in his eyes. He was nowhere near standing beside her. He was far, far away, deep in the cave.

Amacy tried pushing her sleeve up, but it dropped to her wrist. She was hot and unpleasantly sweaty in her fleece pajamas, perfect for Pennsylvania winter, terrible for spelunking in hell. She savagely rolled up both of her sleeves. Who cared if her rage stretched the fabric? She would probably burn this stupid thing when she got back to the surface.

She kept trudging along, despite her hunger, weariness, and stickiness. She needed this to be over so that she could move somewhere remote and never think about sprites and leprechauns and dragons and Tristan ever again. If this was what it took to live with the man of her dreams, she would happily give up and be single for the rest of her life.

Something glowed ahead with the familiar golden glow of Shrew's creations. She hurried forward and found a tiny corn stalk, feebly holding on to life in a place it was never meant to grow. She reached down and touched it, receiving a garbled message about portals opening naturally. Before the vision had even truly ended, it disintegrated, the tiny stalk a pile of dust beneath her hand. What would she have seen if she had found it sooner?

She got to her feet and realized that not far ahead, the corridor bent, leading off in a different direction, the way ahead blocked with rubble.

She peered around the bend and gasped. "Switch off the lantern," she breathed to Tristan, and he did so, joining her.

The tunnel was a few feet long, ending in a room illuminated with the ice-white glow of the flowers and grass. A rush of water hurried somewhere ahead. Somehow, she suspected they'd found where the dragon lived.

She took the lantern from Tristan and set it just out of sight on the other side of the turn, just as Shrew had hidden the light of his little plant.

She looked up at Tristan in the glow not unlike a profusion of Christmas lights and tried to convey without words that this was it, the end, and they had arrived at what they had come for. He looked down at her briefly, then walked away, not even attempting caution.

He was long gone to her.

Following him, she marveled at each expanse of the room beyond as it was revealed to her. White grass and flowers grew in a large field. Out of the wall to the left, a sparkling blue waterfall shimmered and flowed down into a valley in the floor, as though instead of coming to a room in a mine, they had in fact come to an outdoor scene. On the ceiling, high above, bluish white mushrooms glowed down upon them, adding more light to the scene. She stepped out of the tunnel and was surprised to find that there was a gentle breeze coming from somewhere scented with sunshine and pine trees. Neither would ever touch this deep below ground.

Tristan was already somewhere out of sight he was going so fast. Her heart leapt, and she hurried forward as well, over the crest of the grassy hill, and found that the water flowed from the waterfall through a stone arch. It looked like the type found on a castle in a medieval movie.

What is that doing down here?

Tristan strode down the hill toward the arch. Amacy rushed to catch up to him, unwilling to let him just keep haring off willy-nilly without her. She nearly slid down the slick surface of the grass near the water, but she kept her feet and grabbed his arm just as he was about to pass through the doorway into the next room. With merely a disinterested glance, he shook her off and went on.

She paused only a moment before she leapt bodily onto his back. “What is wrong with you?”

She hissed the question into his ear, clinging with both legs and arms to him. He teetered, off balance, and started to fall. She let her legs down and dug in, still holding him with her arms.

“I’m not going to let you just walk into a dragon’s lair with no fight in you. Wake the hell up.”

He leaned against her, stiff as a corpse, for a moment, before regaining his balance and pulling her feet up off the ground again.

“I need to go to him,” he said. “That’s been our plan the entire time.”

“Yes, *our*, not *I*. This is for both of us to do, not just you on your own.”

She thought she saw a moment of realization in his eye as the blue circle on her face was pressed up against his cheek, but a new voice broke around them, startling them both. She slid back to the ground.

“How sweet. Though really, if you two had ever truly been united in anything, perhaps we wouldn’t all be in this mess.”

It was a deep voice, one that spoke of ancient things and sea monsters.

From the room beyond, some gentle whisps of smoke escaped to dance around their feet. “You may as well come in. This is what you came for, as he said.”

Tristan stepped in immediately, and Amacy had to scramble to follow.

The room was large and built from stone, keeping with the castle theme the archway promised. More of the mushrooms grew from the ceiling here, the light subdued without the white light of the grass. To one side, the floor stood broken, a jagged edge above the pooling water of the river. The waters swirled in a glowing vortex before disappearing into a small crack in the wall. Birds sang somewhere beyond. Sunlight filtered through, stabbing in like the husband from *The Shining*.

“What is that?” she couldn’t help herself. The words just came out.

“Somewhere I would desperately love to be.” The voice was closer than she would like, and smoke surrounded them, smelling of summertime barbecues.

She did not want to look, but she did anyway. Lying there against the far wall was a large red dragon, thin and frail-looking. His large golden eyes seemed too large for his long face. The wings at his back were as small and stunted as they had been when he had been young. He was no threat to anyone, just a sad, lonely, half-dead dragon deep below a civilization he could never be a part of.

Amacy sat down hard, tears that had very little to do with the smoke issuing from him running down her cheeks.

They had come here expecting to find a dragon capable of the end of the world. What they found was a dragon at the end of his life.

Send him to me.

The voice seemed to come half from inside her own head, half from the other side of the hole in the wall.

She went to the water's edge and peered into the space. "What is that on the other side?"

Behind her, there was a shifting sound and a metallic clang, and she looked up, only to find the dragon had knocked Tristan to the floor, its beak-like muzzle directly over his throat. Amacy's mouth went dry.

"Salvation," the dragon said. "But it is too small. I knew it was here, even when I was just an egg. Passed between ignorant humans until this one could hear my call."

Instead of taking a mouthful of Tristan's throat, the dragon nuzzled his neck, his huge eyes closed. "He listened to me as I told him to hatch me. And when I was young and couldn't remember what I wanted from life, he gave me to you, who raised me. For which I am eternally grateful. When he released me into the wild, it was all part of my plan. I left the cave the same day and started walking. My wings were made wrong, so I could not fly as I would have liked. It took longer than I had hoped, but I ate well. Pennsylvania is a beautiful land full of largesse for a dragon's stomach."

"So...you didn't start those fires in the mines around Pittsburgh?"

His tone became condescending. "Don't blame monsters for the things humans do to themselves. No, those were corrupt mine companies, not me."

Brasmanathnon lay down full-length next to Tristan, his frail body still twice as long and twice as wide as his. "When I got here, though, this portal was too small. I couldn't get in. Things would come out sometimes. Seeds and sounds. But I could not go in. Sometimes, bad things would come through. Monsters. Men. I had to kill them so that your world was safe. You are too small and squishy to defend against these kinds of things anymore. But then, I sensed you again, Father, and I knew everything would be all right."

He nuzzled Tristan again, who looked disturbingly like a corpse.

"The others told me that you can open the portal further, Mother, if you only remember. And then, when I'm through, you can close it again. Everyone will be safe."

She looked at the little portal, barely large enough for her to fit through. "Are there others like this?"

Brasmanathnon shook his massive head. "No, I don't believe there are any others left. Or I would have tried to get to one of those instead. Will you help me?"

"Shrew and Fiona. Did they make it to you?"

"Yes. And then they left through the portal. They fit, unlike me."

Amacy nodded. That decided what she had to do then. "I'm going after them. There must be a reason they went through."

Brasmanathnon made an unpleasant sound in the back of his throat, then said, "Fine, but I will keep Father with me until you come back."

Tristan lay comatose on the floor still, sword knocked from his reach. She didn't fully trust the dragon, but she didn't believe he would hurt Tristan. At least not on purpose.

"All right. But know this, if he is no longer alive when I return, there will be nothing in your future."

"I wouldn't have it any other way, Mother."

She stepped into the water. It was deeper than it seemed. She was up to her waist in seconds. In her now wet pink fleece pajamas, she entered a new world.

The light was so bright she had to throw up a hand against it. She blinked and found, to her surprise, that despite her inappropriate attire, she felt stronger than she had mere moments ago. Her legs were stronger. Her arms felt like she could lift anything. Her lungs could hold more air. The feeling was intoxicating.

"Good stuff, eh?" The voice was familiar, but she couldn't place it.

She turned, finding a large blue dragon lounging on the bank to her left. "Hey," he said, wiggling his dragon fingers...claws... whatever they were at her, a piece of long grass clenched between his teeth.

"You don't remember me, do you?"

Still up to her knees in cold water, Amacy shook her head. "Only dragon I've met this life is behind that portal. But I can guess. You're Chuck?"

He beamed, at least as much as a dragon face allows for beaming. "You may not recognize me, but you remember I exist. That's enough for me." He waved a beckoning hand at her. "Come on up. You can't be too comfortable standing in that water."

She looked down at her feet, clad in sneakers with no socks, and blushed a little as she climbed the bank of the creek. She sat down on the grass next to him. Strangely, though he was easily twice the size of poor Brasmanathnon, essentially a behemoth next to her, she still felt comfortable.

The sun sparkled off his sapphire blue scales and made the lighter, powder-blue ones on his belly even more translucent, as though his scales from right below his chin to the tip of his tail were made of ice. The tall horns atop his head and the tiny ones at the tip of his nose were a deep cream, almost golden, color, and the darker blue tendrils alongside his mouth looked like a long mustache. He was a beautiful creature.

"I've missed you," he said as she sat wetly next to him.

"I think our current problem has come from the fact that we miss you too."

Chuck *hmmph*ed and chewed on his bit of grass. Which in actuality, now that she was closer, she saw was actually a corn stalk.

Corn stalk.

"Did Shrew and Fiona pass this way?"

"That they did." Chuck grinned. "The corn give it away? He thought it might."

"Where did they go?"

"Why, exploring, of course. They've not felt magic this strong in years. Think of it like you think of someone going to an overpriced open house for the home of their dreams. Pretty sure they're not going to buy it but really want to see it anyway."

The creek babbled pleasantly next to them. It didn't glow out here, but then it really didn't have to. The sun made up for what sparkle the water had lost outside the cave.

"How do I make the rift bigger?"

Chuck laughed. "No one here knows that but you. I might have been your guinea pig last time, but you never told me how you did it. I can't complain too much, as it obviously worked and likely saved my life. This one's already partially open, so much easier, right?"

"Sure," she muttered.

They sat in silence for a while longer. Something screeched overhead and she looked up. The creature had the head of an eagle but the body of a cat...a griffon?

“Don’t worry. He won’t hurt you. Horace is keeping watch. As much as I would like to tell you that everything is ideal here, it’s not. He’s my eyes in the sky, as your weathermen like to say.”

Amacy leapt to her feet, sodden fleece slapping her in the back of the legs. “And Shrew and Fiona are out there?”

Chuck chuckled. “I think you’ll find they are capable of taking care of themselves. Shrew is slightly hindered by how far he is from his main plant, but the amount of magic here is more than enough to make up for it.”

“Main plant?”

Chuck laughed. “Didn’t he tell you? Being a potato sprite is much easier than being a tree sprite. Any little bit of that original potato plant is his plant. He carries a tiny seedling on him at all times so that if anyone gets the big idea to kill his seed potato, he will still have the baby potato with him. Tubers are quite portable."

Maybe being a potato sprite wasn't so lame after all.

"What if they decide to stay here?" It wasn't important to their quest, and she barely knew them, but it made her immeasurably sad to think of never seeing them again.

"Then he'll need his whole potato. I'm glad that you can rationally see that might be an option. But there's another option you're missing."

"What's that?"

Chuck shrugged, then sat up, towering over her. "It'll come to you. Now, Shrew said one of your powers was to get visions from those you touch. Fiona said you wear a necklace that amplifies your magic but dampens the visions. If you take it off and touch me, do you think maybe you could figure out how to rip the rift a little bit more and let my little cousin through?"

“We can try, I suppose,” she said, her heart racing. She reached up and unclasped the necklace with trembling fingers, then handed it to Chuck to hold so it wouldn’t get lost in the grass. Her breath came too quickly, and she felt a little lightheaded. It was then that she realized that her soul loved Chuck and was entwined with him almost as much as she was with Tristan. With overexcited fingers, she touched one of the glassy scales at his stomach.

Chuck lay on the ground before her, emaciated as Brasmanathnon. She could barely see him through the tears in her eyes.

“Don’t be so sad,” he said, his voice a rasp. “You’ll see me again. We always see one another again.”

Amacy sniffled. “You can’t be sure that will be true this time.” She rubbed a hand over his scales and then sighed. “I can’t watch you suffer. I either send you on to a world where we will no longer be connected, or you stay here and die. I don't like this choice."

"I don't either. But be heartened. You have your love. Send me on somewhere I may finally find mine."

The last dragon left. What would it be like to be the last elf? The last human?

She closed her eyes and pulled the power from deep inside her. She felt the other world in the pit of her stomach, and she pulled it out, setting it on the ground next to Chuck.

It glowed, then opened down into a bright world below. Her love and loss fed it. Duality was key. Without light there was no darkness, without love there was no loss.

"Go on, then. Live your life. Find your love. Survive."

Chuck moved painfully to the hole, his wings flexible and feeble. "I know you. Don't go following me. Not yet anyway.

You have too much here. Maybe someday, you can come along when your attachment to this world isn't so tight."

He slid into the hole, head-first, the rest of his body following close behind. When the end of his horn-tipped tail disappeared from view, Amacy took the other world back and placed it inside herself once more.

"I will keep you inside me forever," she said, finally dissolving into tears as her legs let out and she fell to the ground. Tristan came up behind her and put a hand to her shoulder and she leaned heavily against him.

"I promise you one day, we will see him again," he said.

"Don't make promises you can't keep."

"I will do my best to make this a promise that isn't broken."

Amacy gasped and came back to the light of the current day. Chuck stepped away and handed her the necklace.

She put it back on and a large, rough, scaly finger wiped the tears from her cheeks. Then in a supremely awkward gesture, he put his arms around her.

Her arms out wide like hugging an ancient oak tree, Amacy hugged back. “I think I know what I need to do. Is there any way to contact Shrew and Fiona? I want to talk to them before we plan much further.”

“I think so, yes,” Chuck said. If he guessed her plan, he said nothing to her. She pulled back from him and sat back down in the grass, certain her butt was likely as wrinkly as her fingers. Chuck waved down his friend, Horace. He landed with a whuff of wind and a smattering of dust and pebbles. Amacy coughed and brought the hawk eyes to her.

“So, you’re her, huh? Do you know how often he comes out here and pines away, looking into this hole? It's quite distressing, really."

Before Amacy could make a retort, Chuck said, "Come now, Horace. That's not a very kind way to greet someone."

Horace shrugged, a strange gesture for a creature with the head of a bird and the body of a lion.

Chuck sighed. "Just go find the other two and bring them back, will you?"

"That I can do," Horace said, taking off again, the draft from his huge, feathered wings nearly flattening Amacy to the ground.

"He's a bit prickly. Please tell me he's not your boyfriend."

Chuck laughed. "You are always so quick to judge my lovers because they're not perfect. But no, he's not my boyfriend."

"Good," Amacy said.

* * *

Both Shrew and Fiona looked more robust out in the sun of the new world. Amacy could barely recognize them. She was sad to think that their own world didn't have what it took to fill them up like this one could—magic. She didn't want to make them return to the place that made them less, but she must.

"Let's go back to the other side and talk. This involves Tristan too."

Shrew and Fiona shared a wary look. "What is it you're planning on doing?" Fiona's small, Irish-accented voice sounded strange out here in a world so far from Ireland.

"I have an idea, but I think it's important that all involved have a say before I do it."

They looked at one another, then nodded.

"What about me?" Chuck's question made her smile. Impudent as always.

"You can listen at the door if you really want to. I don't think you'll fit."

He shrugged. “Fair enough.”

As much as she didn’t want to go into the water, she forced herself in. The water seemed several times colder than the first time she’d entered it, stealing her breath as it pressed against her in a hug. The water sloshed higher up her body as it tried to flow through her. By the time she got back to where Brasmanathnon lurked, she was chilled in her entirety and it took extra-long for her eyes to get used to the glowing dark. Tristan was awake now, sitting up, talking with Brasmanathnon in hushed tones.

He looked up when he noticed the sounds of the water and smiled. “I was hoping you’d come back. Brasmanathnon and I have been having an interesting discussion. Did you know that our world gets all its magic through this little hole?”

Amacy came in the rest of the way, pulling herself up onto the stonework, her shoes squelching uncomfortably. “I did not.”

"That's the only way he's been able to survive, to live down here near the entrance. This is why there used to be so many more tales of magic and wonder, because there used to be more portals from here to there. This is the last."

Amacy stopped, wet splashing sounds coming from behind her. *All the more reason to have this discussion.*

She went and sat next to Tristan, wet pants even colder against the cold floor. Brasmanathnon lifted his head pitifully, his large eyes making him look more innocent than he was in truth.

"So, what's all this about?" Fiona wasn't even out of the pool yet and already making demands.

"Come sit," Amacy said, preparing what she wanted to say before presenting her thoughts to the group.

They did so, eyeing her suspiciously.

“I think I can open the rift farther in order to get Brasmanathnon out,” she said. “But then afterward, I’d like to close it to keep the world safe.”

“But what about magic?” Tristan shouted it out before anyone else even seemed to process what she’d said. “What about Shrew and Fiona? What about the fairies in the snow? Wouldn’t that kill them all?”

“No,” said Shrew softly. “It wouldn’t kill us. Existing magic would remain, but no new magic would be born. If you closed it off and lived a normal life and died, you would no longer be reborn with your memories. You would be reborn as regular humans. The chances of finding one another again would be small.”

Tristan looked away, frowning. “I don’t know that I am all right with that. What is life if there is no magic in it?”

“Most people believe that there already is no magic in it. It’s already mostly gone.

You and I mere days ago believed it wasn't real," Amacy said.

He looked away from her.

"There is a second part to my suggestion. I believe we should gather up everything that's important to us and stay on the other side."

Shrew nodded in approval and got up immediately. Fiona stayed put, either dissenting or having nothing she wanted.

"Stay on the other side?" Tristan sputtered.

"I know you can't really understand because you haven't been out there, but after seeing what things *could* be like, I don't want to live in a world without magic anymore. I would love to continue our lives in the world we know. I have family, friends, a job. But after being out there, just nothing compares. We can't selfishly leave this rift open to allow magic to trickle in to keep our lives the same, because once we release Brasmanathnon, he won't be here to stop anything malicious that wishes to come through. You can't look at him and suggest to me that we just leave things the way they are!"

Tristan shook his head. "You're right. I am being selfish. Can I…can I go out and at least experience it before I exile myself there for the sake of the world?"

It was a true testament to the entwining of their souls that he didn't even once suggest she go without him.

They looked over to Brasmanathnon who nodded. "But this time, Mother stays with me."

"I'm going to go get my potato," Shrew announced and walked away.

Fiona stayed put. Amacy eyed Brasmanathnon with his hanging jowls of empty skin and his too-big eyes and was glad she wouldn't be left alone with him. Anything bigger than she was and calling her "Mother" was enough to freak her out.

“That’s fine,” she said, even though it really wasn’t.

Tristan stepped through the portal, the cold water clearing his mind to a degree he wasn’t sure he had felt in this lifetime. He let the sun rain down on him like a waterfall of heat and light, cleansing the last cobwebs of someone else’s influence from his soul.

How long had Brasmanathnon been fiddling with his mind? He wondered how much of his “illness” had been influenced by the dragon’s touch.

Brasmanathnon had made him who he was this life and the last. He was aware of that now, after their time together in the cave. The dragon hadn’t come out and said as much, but Tristan had felt that presence deepen as he walked down the stone hallways. That presence that had always been there, making him second-guess everything he'd ever done.

Tristan wanted freedom and he knew the best way to make sure no one else ever had a chance to influence his mind would be to stay on the side of the portal that did not have magic in it. But Amacy wanted to stay here, and he wished wholeheartedly to be where she was.

“Horace could have eaten you eight times. Good thing he's friendly.”

Tristan jumped then lost his footing on the slippery stones in the bed of the little pool, splashing to his neck in cold water. He sputtered as he tracked the source of the deep laughter, as he took off his soaked glasses and pushed his wet hair out of his face.

A dragon sat on the bank, laughing his little reptilian heart out. And what did Tristan really expect? Reptiles were cold-hearted creatures. Or cold-blooded. One of those.

Tristan got up, soaked to his skin in his button-down and slacks and nice shoes and no socks. He wiped his glasses fruitlessly on his wet shirt and replaced them on his nose. "Chuck, I presume?"

"I sure missed you, kid," Chuck said. "Come sit with me for a while. Seems I get to hang out with all my favorite people today."

Tristan squelched to the bank and sat next to Chuck. "Well, if Amacy has her way, you will be having even more days with your favorite people."

"I heard," Chuck said, not even trying to hide his enthusiasm.

"I don't know that she's really thought it through. This place is...nice but ,we know nothing about it. She was out here for a few minutes, and now she wants to spend the rest of whatever lives we have here?"

"Sometimes desires are more important than logic. If you don't take this opportunity now, you will never have the chance again. You will forever be trapped in a magic-less world. What do you really have back in your world that you need to keep?"

"My life was *finally* going right for me. I had money and a real home for the first time since...well, ever. Mom had a hard time making enough money to keep us housed, and I wouldn't call the revolving apartments I grew up in homes. But suddenly, I had acceptance. I think I had love."

"And you had adventure. Really, Tristan, are you going to tell me you're the kind of man who prizes *things* over the important stuff? Where does your acceptance go in a world where no one can be born with magic? Where does your love go if you choose to stay while she leaves? Where does your adventure go if you stay on your behind drinking tea in someone else's kitchen for the rest of your life, living off their money?"

Tristan felt as though he had been slapped across the face. He'd been thinking of it as almost an ultimatum from Amacy—her or the world he loved. But Chuck was right. He had been looking at it all wrong. The only things that the world behind had to offer him were material things and creature comforts. Yes, things would be harder here, but maybe harder was something he needed more of in his life. A fresh start. A true fresh start. Somewhere no one at all knew him except the people who already loved him.

"Will I be free of Brasmanathnon's influence here?"

"Seems you already are, aren't you?"

"True. What do you think made him choose to use me like that?"

Chuck leaned back on his elbows and stared into the sky before replying. "Have you ever been the last of anything?"

Tristan's heart sank. "Is he truly the last? Will we accidentally trap others in the world without magic when we close this last portal?"

Chuck stared at Tristan for a moment, then smiled. "How unselfish of you. Perhaps I'm getting through to you a little. And because you said that on your own, I will reward you. Did you know that if your lovely lady in there can open a portal from your world to mine, she can also open a portal from my world to yours? You are perfectly free to decide to go home at any time, even if that means that your decision will be permanent."

Irritated, Tristan said, "Why didn't you tell me this before?"

Chuck shrugged. "Well, because you were being a jerk and you had to realize that what you had with my best friend was more important than money and things."

The laugh that escaped Tristan's mouth felt as though it had been ripped from deep within, a pleasant thing, a certain thing. He couldn't remember the last time he'd been certain of anything. The sun, the water, and the company made everything so much more correct in his mind. "I guess I'd best go back and tell her that I'm all right with staying. We will have plenty of time to talk and reacquaint ourselves with one another from now on."

"Oh, this will be fun. I'll be able to try all my tricks on you again because you won't remember them," Chuck shouted after him as he ducked back through the hole.

Amacy watched Tristan come back from the other world, and she could see wisps of golden light dissipating from him like steam from a road in summer. He was so beautiful, and his limbs seemed to be filled with a vigor she had never seen in him. His head did not bow in shyness even though his wet shirt clung to his body. And she loved him all the more for it.

“So, maybe we’ll stay,” Tristan said, and Amacy cheered, then got up from where she sat next to the wrinkled form of Brasmanathnon and ran to him. He still stood in the water, so she was taller than him for once. She took the opportunity to wrap her arms around his neck and kiss him on the mouth. It was their first unhindered kiss, a kiss of affection and nothing more. No more confusion, no more uncertainty. Her body and his were meant to be together just the same as their souls always had been.

“About damn time,” Fiona said, making Amacy turn to her once more. She still sat huddled in the corner like she felt ill.

“What do you mean?” Though she kept her tone light, there had been some venom interjected into Fiona’s words.

“Exactly what I said. We’ve known about natural portals for some time. We’ve tried to get you to go before. But every time it was always, ‘But what if something happens in the world where they need us?' I'm glad that you've finally gotten over your selfish thought that you two are the only ones good enough to save the Earth. Just because we've done it together a time or two doesn't mean that we need to do it forever. It's someone else's turn."

Amacy frowned, a tiny bit of ice piercing her heart. She hadn't thought of the fate of the world if they left it. But she also knew deep inside that they wouldn't be needed again. Anything left wouldn't be big enough a problem to humanity after living with it for so long, and nothing new could come. She forced a smile. "Maybe we just needed to wait until we were sure nothing else would hurt it if we left."

Fiona laughed, having left her sharpness behind. "That sounds just like something you would say. If Shrew would hurry up, we could get on with the rest of our lives."

"I don't think he really needs to be back for me to open it enough for Brasmanathnon through. It must be murder on him to see us coming and going. I think it's his turn."

She smiled at him, but the way he was looking at her made the expression slip. His eyes held a hunger that left her uncomfortable. She just couldn't bring herself to trust him. Even though he was a sorrowful heap who could barely lift his overlarge head.

She moved toward the door. "I can probably do it from in here," she said, suddenly unwilling to leave the dragon alone with people she cared about.

"Are you sure it will work from in here?" Brasmanathnon's voice was high and raspy, but something rang false.

When she glanced over to him, however, all she could read was concern. She stopped herself from shaking her head to clear it. More than likely, he would misconstrue it as an answer.

"I'm not, but I'm sure going to try."

Amacy sat on the stones of the floor, looking at the hole that led from one world to another. She still wasn't completely certain how this magic thing worked, but Fiona had suggested that it was based on desires, and the memories that she had gleaned from Chuck made it feel like she had just pulled it out of herself, fully formed. She remembered the exhaustion that came with it. But she was among friends. She had others to look after her if she took too much out.

But still. "Pick up your sword, Tristan. You don't want to leave it here."

A scrape of metal behind her told her he had complied.

She put out her hands and grasped the rock at the top of the ragged edge of the portal, her fingers dug deep into the dirt of the little hill outside. With an effort having more to do with strain from within than from her arms, she began to pull up. It moved, but her muscles became weak quickly. Her chest felt like rubber. But she had to keep going. Slowly, she kept pulling up and smoothing out as she stood to make it taller. She sent it out to the sides to make it wider as well. It was so tiring, but it wasn't big enough yet. Her legs began to shake.

Hands touched her waist, and then Tristan's arms pulled her to him, lending his body's strength to her to hold her up. She continued expanding, the blue glow of the mushrooms and the water dimming as the sunlight from the outside became the sunlight inside. Finally, most of the wall was open to the other side. She leaned back against Tristan, her body sagging, her breath coming as though she had just run a sprint.

"It's done," she said between pants. "Brasmanathnon, welcome to your new home."

There was no sound from the back of the room where Brasmanathnon lay, not a breath, not a squeak of thank-you. Had he expired while she worked? She was about to turn to look when something hit both her and Tristan hard from behind. Tristan took the brunt of it, but it knocked them both to the ground.

“Why did you do this to me?” the voice hissed from above.

Amacy’s head was ringing. She was too weak to get up. She thought she’d done what he’d wanted. He’d said he wanted out.

Another blow came and Tristan was thrown off her. She was going to die, and she didn’t know why.

“You abandoned me! We were a family, and you threw me out like I was trash! TRASH!” He was screaming in his horrible hissing voice. The sound bored directly into her eardrums.

She pushed herself to her elbows and stared at the dragon. “You said you wanted to come here, that you wanted us to leave you so you could do so.”

"Those are the words you wanted to hear. I wanted to live, and I wanted to live *here*, where I'm special. Now that you've opened the portal wider, I can come and go as I please and I can live here, where the world is ripe for the picking by the strong. You won't be making it back or leaving for the other side, though. You're the only one who can close this, and I just can't let that happen."

Brasmanathnon reared back, no longer looking weak or ineffective. And then Tristan was in front of her, empty-handed but willing to protect her anyway.

He must have left the sword when he came to hold me up.

As Tristan lunged at the dragon, shoulder-first, attempting to bowl over his larger opponent, Amacy saw the glitter of the sword. Fiona, who had been sitting next to the dragon was struggling to bring the large sword to bear. While Tristan grappled the dragon, Fiona grappled with the sword.

Brasmanathnon's hands tore at Tristan's shoulders. His claws, though mercifully blunted by walking on stone, still ripped rivulets of blood from him. His shirt was in tatters. Fiona finally lifted the sword and stabbed Brasmanathnon through the foot. He howled, hugging Tristan even closer, ripping a shout of pain from him as well.

And that was when Shrew walked through the door, a mystified expression on his face, a huge cement planter in his hands. Without seeming to take a moment of thought for his plant growing inside, he took two long strides and smashed the pot into Brasmanathnon's face. The pot shattered, and the plant spilled out, but Brasmanathnon's arms went limp as well and Tristan rolled to the floor, gasping and holding his ribs.

Shrew caught his plant before it could fall to the stone floor. He cradled it to his body. Its golden glow had returned, so it seemed it would survive its traumatic day.

“Chuck,” Shrew bellowed, striding across the floor to the opening, leaving a trail of dirt leading from the dragon’s face. At the entrance, he shouted, “Come in here and get this bastard before he wakes up and tries to kill us again!”

Chuck’s concerned face appeared almost at once. His large silver eyes took in the damage and sighed. “You miserable bastard.” he said, “You give all dragons a bad name.”

He reached in an arm and snagged Brasmanathnon’s tail, then dragged him from the cold, dark room into the sunlight.

“You all had best get out here too,” he said, his voice getting quieter as he got farther away. “If you’ll remember, I’m a healer, so I can take a look at your various injuries.”

Shrew helped Tristan to his feet, then came over and lifted Amacy in a one-armed scoop.

“What kind of fertilizer are you giving that plant?” Her question came out muzzily, hazed with sleep. She was going to give over to it soon, she was sure.

“Adventure. It’s the best fertilizer for anything.”

Chapter 14

Home

Tristan sat and watched the water rush out of the portal to the world he planned to leave as a dragon washed the lacerations on his back with some kind of herbal concoction. Last week, no doubt, he would have been the only one to think the doctor operating on him resembled a giant lizard. This week, everyone could see the giant lizard. Behind them, a griffon stood watch over a still unconscious creature who had called him "Father" then tried to kill him. Life was a strange thing.

No doubt his contemplative feeling had something to do with the tea Chuck had given him, but he wasn't going to question it. He was feeling pretty good despite having been roughed-up mere moments ago.

A few feet away, Amacy slept in the grass near the bank of the water. He longed to go stretch out next to her and breathe in the lilac scent of her until the end of time, but he had a feeling that when the pain came back, he wouldn't want to be lying flat on the ground.

He asked the group at large, "Where will we go from here?"

Chuck paused. "Anywhere." Tristan could hear the joy in his voice.

"Not every day will be like this here, right?"

Chuck didn't answer right away. "Not *every* day, per se. Horace and I could find you a nice place that is safe and cozy and warm, and you will never have days like this again. But...that is an awfully nice sword you have there. So, you do have options after all. And from what Fiona said, you are a vicious little bastard when you want to be."

Tristan laughed. "I don't want to be a vicious little bastard every day, though."

Chuck shrugged. "Your loss."

They sat for a while in the bright sunlight, birds chirping some ways away. "I guess we will leave it up to Amacy," he said finally.

"Safe choice. Well, you're all done. Feel free to explore while our lady sleeps off her magic hangover."

"But what about you? What have you been doing since we saw you last? You don't seem to have aged at all."

Chuck shrugged again, then said, "Come with while I see to your creepy buddy over here, and I'll tell you."

So, Tristan followed Chuck over to Brasmanathnon.

“I’m not lonely anymore,” Chuck said. “I’ve been here for a long time, and I’ve been reborn a few times. But like you, I remember. I’m still your Chuck, through and through.”

He sat down and inspected the foot that Fiona had stabbed.

“Many years ago, I took part in a campaign to save this world. Lucky for you, I’m still here to tell the tale. I found a boyfriend too, at long last. He was a hottie. Ah, well. Not everyone is reborn after they die. If a life is fulfilling enough, they move on. They’re done with the cycle. Just look at us twerps who refuse to fall into that category, though.” He laughed.

“You weren’t satisfied?”

“Heavens, no. I hadn’t safely ushered you into this world yet, a place where I knew you would be happier. This is probably finally the last life for me. And maybe for you as well. We shall see."

Tristan watched as Chuck washed the foot, then medicated it and wrapped it. "We'll have to figure out what to do with this friend of yours. He's a bit messed up in the head if you hadn't noticed."

Snorting, Tristan said, "Master of the understatement as always. I don't want to kill him. He deserves the chance to live a satisfying life now that he has a whole new world to explore."

"Agreed. But it doesn't change the fact that he is dangerous. We should get that portal closed as soon as possible as well. As long as it's here, he has the chance to try it again. As soon as it is closed and he understands that Amacy is the only one who can open them again, you will be safe. He won't risk killing the only person who could fulfill his nasty dream for him."

"I suppose that's true."

"We can give Amacy some time to sleep, though. And you look half-dead as well. Why don't you join her for a while? Horace and I will keep you safe."

Tristan nodded, his head feeling thick and fuzzy as he did so. Sleep seemed like a gloriously good idea.

He wandered down the bank and lay next to her, rolling onto his side to keep his mangled shoulders out of the dirt. Even in her dirty pink fleece pajamas, Amacy was the most beautiful woman he knew, and he curled into her, his face in her hair, breathing her scent, his arm across her body.

He could lie like this forever. Even if he knew it really wasn't possible.

When Amacy opened her eyes once more, the sun had gone down. The moon was bright enough to illuminate her surroundings, but dim enough to allow the glow of the mushrooms from her old world to sparkle in all their blue glory once more. Insects chirruped around her, a pleasantly familiar and comforting sound. Her new home was a lovely world.

Behind her, Tristan murmured in his sleep and momentarily grasped her more tightly. She wanted to stay next to him, but she also knew that everyone would be safer once she closed the portal. It was time.

She gently moved Tristan's arm from her body and kissed his scraped knuckles before levering herself off the ground. She walked across the grass, a sorceress in pink fleece and sneakers, and took a last long look at the world they were leaving behind. It was a good, functional sort of place. But it was also somewhere none of them belonged anymore. They needed a realm of magic and wonder, of adventure and the new. And they would have it here, learning new things with their oldest friends, living their lives in a way that gave them more than just the money to survive another day. No longer would she eke out an existence in a world where what was acceptable was defined by how many dollars it cost. Her heart soared in her chest.

Reaching up, she grasped the lip of the portal and was about to pull it down, to shrink it to nothing, when she remembered her vision, her memory of the time she had sent Chuck away to live his life.

Reaching out, she instead took the portal and pulled it inside. The opening collapsed and disappeared, the water stopping its flow for a moment before starting back up from whatever spring had fed it from this side. She would keep the portal inside herself forever, just in case they ever needed it again to return.

She turned and looked back to where the others slept. Shrew lay curled around his plant, if at all possible, taller than he had been in Pennsylvania. Fiona, a minuscule child by his side, no longer looked like an overworked bar owner, cross with everyone. She smiled in her sleep.

Chuck slept nearby, sprawled like a toddler, crushing a small tree without even noticing. Horace sat on Brasmanathnon's chest, looking grumpy. He nodded in her direction in acknowledgement that he had seen her.

Amacy nodded back, then walked back to where Tristan was and lay next to him again. It was going to be a good life here with him and all their friends.

Epilogue

Sometimes endings are just endings. Others are the opportunities for new beginnings. This one, though…this one is a middle with lives stretching forward and back from this point in time forever and ever.

Tristan walked down the trail, Chris, his youngest son, strapped to his back, a walking stick in hand. His little head leaned against Tristan's back. It felt good. A real, true family. Even if it was a weird family, consisting of three rambunctious children, a mother, a father, two aunts, two uncles, and a host of friends who just showed up whenever they felt like.

The two older children were at home with their mother, being given a rest from the demands of a toddler. They were apparently going to learn dragon-knitting from Chuck to make a wedding gift for Aunt Fiona who would be marrying her sweetheart, Brioche, a fairy. The wedding was only a few days away, and it had been decided that daddy and baby were only in the way, so they should go off and do something on their own.

Tristan didn't mind. Today, he was on a mission.

He climbed an uneven section of rock following alongside the little creek he had been tracing for the last few miles. He would find where they were going eventually. He would maybe get home by dark. And if he wasn't, well, surely big Uncle Chuck would come out and find them and rescue them and bring them home.

The forest was calm and still that day, nothing but the breeze in the leaves of the trees above and the gentle babble of the brook below. The banks were wider than the water they contained, the dry sections hanging over the rich soil of the bed. Logs were overgrown with moss and fungus. It was beautiful.

Chris hiccupped behind him. He would wake soon and they would take a break so that Chris could have a snack and maybe walk a little on his own before he got too cranky and insisted on being carried.

But not yet. He had a little more time. A bird shot out of the undergrowth ahead, startling him. It twittered at him then flew off into the sky. Chris coughed and said, “Daddy?”

So much for time. “Did you have a good nap?”

“Mmhmm. Fruit please?”

"Let me stop and get you out. I have some dried apricots in my bag here. We can eat in a minute."

"Like fruit."

He crouched down and unwrapped his son from his back, letting the little boy free, his legs still chubby and soft. He wobbled a few seconds before plonking down on his butt in the dirt, holding his fat little hands out for his treat.

Tristan obliged, giving him a little chunk of dried apricot. "Remember to suck on it a little to soften it before you take a bite off. Little bites. You don't have many teeth."

They sat together in companionable silence, chewing up minuscule amounts of fruit in the middle of the forest, miles away from any town. And they'd go miles more if they could take it.

A few squirrels wandered past while they ate, but nothing horribly untoward happened, and when they were done, they got up. Tristan extended a hand down to his son, and they wandered along the dry creek bed together. The surface was mostly flat and not too hard for tiny feet to walk on. He had to lift Chris over two logs, but the little boy thought it great fun and thought maybe Daddy should carry him like that all the time. And so, the time for walking separately was over, and Tristan re-wrapped the bands that had held Chris to his back, but this time strapped him to his chest.

“Where we goin’, Daddy?” Chris tried to catch the dangling ends of Tristan’s hair that hadn’t been caught in the tail at the back of his head.

“We are going someplace Daddy hasn’t been in a long time. Mommy and I were here years ago together, but we’ve not been back since.”

“Oh,” said Chris, leaning down to look into the water, making it hard for Tristan to balance. “What you think they making?”

It took Tristan a moment to realize his son was not asking about some unseen newts and salamanders but what his other family members were doing at home. "I'm not sure. I think it's an afghan?"

"What's afghan?"

"It's a warm blanket made of yarn."

"Yarn banket!"

They laughed for a bit together then sang some songs together, all the while traveling uphill while the rivulet of water dwindled.

And then they came to the pool. The sun of late afternoon sparkled off the surface of the water, dazzling his eyes.

"Daddy, splash!"

"Probably not, Chris. We have to go all the way back too, and I don't look forward to having to carry you wet."

The place had not changed much, except for the level of the water in the pool. It was lower than when he had last been here, years ago. He didn't think it would come up to his shoulders if he fell in it today. He sat down on the upper bank to unstrap Chris, which was probably a horrible idea, as he still seemed utterly certain splashing was the answer to all of life's tricky questions.

As expected, Chris approached the edge of the water immediately.

He got up and followed his son.

"Not splashin'," Chris said hurriedly. "Just lookin'."

Chris did not lie. His little shoes were *just* outside the pool, *just* not touching it. But he was close enough Tristan felt the need to be at his side anyway.

They both leaned over and looked in the clear water. The first few inches had recently overcome the edge of where it had been before, covering the green plants at the edge. They still showed greenly through the surface, though staying underwater no doubt meant their eventual death. Had it rained recently?

Not really. An uneasy feeling came over Tristan as he looked toward the little cave that the trickle poured from, that spot where the portal had once been. Was that a dim glow? Did he detect a hint of blue?

He leaned down, the tips of his hair touching the water. Below the surface, all the way in the back, a blue mushroom glowed.

Tristan's heart hammered, and he reared back, grabbing his son as he did so.

"Didn't do anything bad, Daddy!"

"I know," he said, as he attempted to strap the struggling toddler to his chest once more. "I'm sorry. It's not your fault. There was just a sudden change of plans."

"Don't like changes, Daddy."

Neither do I, Tristan thought. He glanced over his shoulder as he hurried back away down the hill the way he had come, wondering what the mushroom meant. The ones in the cave on the far side had glowed because of the magic in their world, right?

He tried to convince himself that the mushroom meant nothing.

But he knew in his soul that it didn't. Far from nothing, that mushroom meant *everything*. And none of it good.

* * *

Amacy's concentration on her task broke as Tristan hurried through the front door, Chris gasping happily on his chest. "Daddy run! Daddy run fast!"

Amacy stood up, the large loops of yarn in her hands dropping to the floor. "You were supposed to be gone for a while yet. What's wrong?"

Tristan held up a hand, panting. He crouched to one knee and released their son from his bonds, where he immediately ran over and began pulling at the threads of their partially finished afghan. It was a mark of how worried Amacy was that she didn't say anything about Chris's destruction of her work, but merely waited for Tristan to catch his breath.

"It must be important for you to run. I know you're winded, but you're also worrying me. Recover faster."

Tristan nodded and held up a hand, the gasps coming slower. He licked his lips. "I went up to the place we came through," he said. "I was curious to see it after all these years. It was supposed to be a pleasant day in the woods."

"But what?" Amacy was becoming exasperated.

"When we got to the pool, it looked like maybe the water level had risen recently. But there hasn't been more rain than usual."

Amacy waved a hand dismissively. "That doesn't mean anything. That's spring water. Maybe it rained a lot somewhere else and we're just getting the hind end of it in a slight rising of a water level here. Is that all that's gotten you worked up?"

Tristan shook his head. "No, no, it's not. In the dark under the lip of the overhang over the source, the water glowed blue. When I looked closer, I saw a blue mushroom glowing from somewhere in behind."

Amacy's mouth clapped shut. Anxiety began to pump in her belly. "Those mushrooms came from our side, right? Not the other?"

"Could be, but have you ever seen one out here?"

No, she hadn't, but she really didn't want to admit it. "Spores could have come through from that side at any point," she said instead. "We could have even tracked them out."

"In the water? How long would a mushroom last underwater?"

That shut her mouth again. She wasn't liking how this was going. She looked over to Chuck, where he sat in his human form, elegant blue hair falling down past his shoulders, his clothes impeccable.

"New plan," she said. "You and the kids finish the afghan and Chuck and I will fly up and take a look and have all this done and over with. The kids have a pretty good handle on it. You just make sure Chris doesn't undo everything."

Tristan nodded and quickly scooped up Chris, removing him from anywhere near the work. "I have an idea," he said, heading toward the bathroom. "How about we go splash in the tub?"

"Splash!"

Amacy smiled. He was so good with the kids. It was a true blessing they could finally have some.

"Emma, Eric, get what you can get done. I'll help you finish it when I get back."

Two little heads nodded. They had been blessed with twins right out of the gate, and it had been wonderful to have so many extra hands to help raise them. They were nine now and old enough to trust to finish a task.

Chuck, got up from his position on the afghan and followed her out of the house. “I suppose you want me to turn scales so you can hitch a ride?”

“If you’d be so kind.”

“It is quite demeaning to strip in your yard every time you want to go adventuring. Someday, I’m going to be standing here starkers and someone will come to visit.”

“If that ever happens, may he be handsome and single,” she said with a laugh.

“That is the dream,” he said, fabric rustling behind her.

Moments later, his large, scaled nose pushed out next to her and he looked up at her with his big silver eyes. “Your beast of burden awaits.”

She went down to the space right above his wings along his long neck and straddled it. “Ready,” she said.

His large blue leathery wings clapped behind her like sails coming to, and they lifted off the ground.

Below them, the house shrank away and then was replaced by trees. Chuck flew along, following the clearly delineated sinuous path of the creek that ran through their back yard, chosen for its proximity to town but also for its position along that very creek. Any reminder of the time they lived in another place was nostalgic, though she was pretty certain neither of them ever truly wanted to go back. Their choice had been based on memories, not on longing. Or so she had thought. Now, with Tristan’s wild tales of mushrooms and glowing water, she wasn’t so sure.

They soared along above the trees, the mountains in the distance where the spring undoubtedly fed from, loomed large. They were lovely, but every time they saw them, Chuck grew melancholy, and she was sorry for having to steer him toward them now. Down below, the trees opened into a meadow and Chuck began spiraling down.

“We’re here,” he said.

“I can see that,” she replied.

The wind of his descent whipped at her ears, making her temporarily deaf.

The land below hurried up to greet them, and he landed surprisingly softly. She dismounted with shaking legs, as she always did when they flew together. The heights were always dizzying and exhilarating, and her body couldn’t seem to choose which one to feel more.

She approached the little pool with anticipation as much as caution, and as the sun had already darkened here, set early by the mountains nearby, she could see the blue glow right away.

Damn. She had hoped that he was just overreacting, seeing things that weren't there in a desire for different times.

She crouched down onto her knees and looked into the little cave they had entered this world through so many years ago, and there the mushroom sat in all its glory, looking for all the world as though it was underwater.

But it wasn't. It was attached to a ceiling on the other side that had absolutely nothing to do with the world they were living in now.

"Damn," she said, lifting her head. "A portal is opening on its own. And I have no idea where it leads to. It looks like the cave on Earth, but it *feels* different."

She got to her feet and held out a hand to Chuck. "Care to explore?

www.ingramcontent.com/pod-product-compliance
Lightning Source LLC
Chambersburg PA
CBHW030340310726
48979CB00001B/121

9781737052920